Metaphorosis

January 2022

Beautifully made speculative fiction

Also from Metaphorosis

Verdage

Reading 5X5 x2: Duets
Score – an SFF symphony
Reading 5X5: Readers' Edition
Reading 5X5: Writers' Edition

Vestige

The Nocturnals by Mariah Montoya

Metaphorosis Magazine

Metaphorosis: Best of 20xx
Metaphorosis 20xx: The Complete Stories
annual issues, from 2016

Monthly issues

Plant Based Press

Best Vegan Science Fiction & Fantasy
annual issues, 2016-2020

from B. Morris Allen:
Chambers of the Heart: speculative stories
Susurrus
Allenthology: Volume I
Tocsin: and other stories
Start with Stones: collected stories
Metaphorosis: a collection of stories

Metaphorosis

January 2022

edited by
B. Morris Allen

ISSN: 2573-136X (online)
ISBN: 978-1-64076-220-6 (e-book)
ISBN: 978-1-64076-221-3 (paperback)

Metaphorosis
a magazine of speculative fiction
from
Metaphorosis Publishing

Neskowin

January 2022

My Synthetic Soul

Karris Rae

The woman who built me is named Tasha. I say "Tasha" so often it feels more familiar than my own name—Jade. Tasha says the sky turns deep jade before a midnight thunderstorm. When it rains hard like that, she sits on the porch steps with a glass of Merlot, watching. Sometimes a gust of wind blows the rain under the eaves and she gets wet, but she never scoots back. She has to be as close as possible, even if she leaves wet footprints on the way to the shower afterward.

Tasha named me after the jade storms —after her second-favorite thing. The first is me. If I weren't, maybe I could join her. But I'm her favorite, so she never lets me outside, not even onto the porch. "You might get hurt," she says, "and I can't fix everything."

There's a storm forecast tonight, too. Tasha's doing yardwork before it hits, on the side of the house I can't see. While I wait for her to come inside and watch the thunderheads roll in with me, I amuse myself with the alternating drama and tedium beyond the bay window—the maids and nannies bustling around the surrounding yards, hanging up laundry, watching human children play. Most are gynoids like me, but some are androids. Tasha works for the company that made the first gynoids, and now every manufacturer borrows from her designs. None outside are human; I've never seen a human carry a mop or hang up the laundry to dry, except for Tasha, who does all the chores for our house.

In fact, my entire life is a backward version of the outside world. Tasha and I argue and giggle together every day, unlike the stoic gynoids outside. And I don't do chores, but I sing while she does hers. All kinds of songs—gentle, spiteful, and reminiscent, but universally melancholic. The kind sung by a doll who watches the world through a pane of glass. They come to me as if pulled, whole, out of the murk of my subconscious, then thrown into the air to take flight. Tasha hums the harmony, even when I'm making the song up in the moment. She's uncanny like that.

I twist my finger around the pull cords of the blinds and close my eyes, singing softly. I experimentally bend the notes, finding spaces between the twelve chromatic scale steps. My vibrato grows wide, wild, and vibrant, testing the limit between exoticism and nonsense. Even now, I bet Tasha could harmonize.

I stop. For a moment, I thought I heard Tasha singing with me from the yard, but there's no way she could hear me from outside. It's a sturdy home; with the windows closed, even violent storms can pass unnoticed.

I cock my head, listening for the second voice, and it rises smoothly out of the silence as if knowing it holds my rapt attention. I don't recognize the song, but I know the voice. It's mine. The notes crawl lightly over my skin like fingers, leaving goosebumps in their wake. Unlike the practical gynoids programmed for work,

Tasha gave me human sensations like these, along with a will of my own. I must be the most overengineered doll in the world. Another human experience seizes my mind—deja vu. I hum and discover that I can place the harmony as well as Tasha.

I'm jealous. Everything else I do might be scripted, programmed, artificial... but music like mine comes from the soul. It's proof that I'm more than a tape recorder who can hiccup. I have to know who else possesses my voice, and why—and if anyone knows, it's Tasha.

I rise from my place on the window seat and cross the over-furnished study, then the dining room. Our home is an anachronistic blend of cutting-edge technology and heavy, dated furniture. I step around the bulky dining table and reach the kitchen. The music is loudest in this corner of the house, but there are no windows between the dark wooden cabinets and the countertops for me to see into the yard. I move the dusty curtains in the dining room aside and press my cheek to the window, where my silicone skin sticks to the glass. This angle affords only a narrow view of the back of the lot, just the blue siding and the sunflowers growing near the foundation. I flip the latch open and crack the window, welcoming in birdsong and the whine of a distant lawnmower. My hearts pounds a little too hard for what should be a simple task.

"Tasha?" I call in a small voice. Why am I so anxious? For as long as I remember, Tasha's never given me a reason to fear her. Besides, curiosity isn't against the rules. The next time I pull strength from deep in my belly, as if reaching the climax of a gospel. "Tasha?"

At the same time, the facsimile of my voice rises in a spellbinding cadenza. Then it tapers into silence. A sound interrupts like I've heard on the funny television shows I sometimes watch with Tasha—applause. Someone, *many* someones, are applauding my performance of a song I've never heard.

Tasha still doesn't answer, but the silence doesn't last long. Another piece starts, just as mystifying as the last. Now that I'm by the open window, I realize I've been looking in the wrong place; the music isn't coming from outside, but from the kitchen itself. I follow the sound to the kitchen, gently touching the softly glowing painting of soap bubbles above the sink. It vibrates under my fingers. It's a subtle invention of Tasha's—a pane of glass over a wide, flat speaker, backlit on either side to illuminate the sink while she loads the dishwasher. The soap bubbles painted over the glass are my addition. Usually the bubbles read us books and play old jazz, but today, they sing me a lullaby in my own voice.

Tasha controls the panel, like everything else in the house... which means if it's playing my music, she commanded it to. I could wait for her to come back inside to ask about it, but the thought of listening to this all afternoon is maddening. And I already tried the window. I teeter in the kitchen, desperate to know why I'm singing to myself, but hesitant to disobey and find out. I've broken rules before, small ones, like licking the rim of Tasha's wine glass while her back was turned. She laughed when she saw the garnet stain on my guilty lips, shaking her head in mock disapproval. Even so, I never did it again. I can't bear to disappoint her, even in jest.

I brace myself, my hand on the doorknob leading to the back yard. When this song ends, the audio skips for a moment, and then it plays again from the beginning. It's a quiet one, intimate, as if I were whispering secrets into my own ear. Surely Tasha, my Creator, will understand why I had to do this. She always does. My synthetic heart beats hard in my aluminum ribcage as I open the door.

The sun overwhelms me. The heat feels like the steam that rises from Tasha's piping hot coffee, but everywhere. I wasn't made to come outside, and I'm more delicate than I guessed.

"What're you doing outside?" I can't see Tasha, but I hear her heavy footsteps crunch on the grass until her hand claps onto my shoulder. "Dammit girl, the heat out here'll put your voice box through hell. Get back in there." She tries to frog-march me back into the kitchen, but I step out of her reach, shielding my eyes with my hands.

"There's music playing in the kitchen... my music," I say, blinking furiously. The quiet song floats out through the open door, into a flurry of distant traffic, birdsong, and rustling leaves.

I see the code running behind Tasha's brown eyes as she puts the pieces together. "Goddammit," she grunts after a minute. "Didn't realize it was broadcasting into the house, too. Goes to show you how bad the UI is, even the 'experts' can't figure it out."

"Who's that singing?" I press. I've heard her gripe about the music software before and know it won't stop.

"It's you," she says, sighing. The logical scripts running in my mind crunch together like trains at a railroad junction. Tasha drops her hand from my shoulder and turns toward the hidden back corner of the lot. She takes a few steps, her gait made uneven by the gout in her left knee. For a moment I think she's abandoned our conversation, but then she says over her shoulder, "Come on, I'll show you."

I follow. My ears can't quite adjust to the unfamiliar white noise that washes over me, sounds diffused over distance until it sounds like the world is shushing me. Tasha says something I don't catch, and then we're standing in front of a shed with no windows. She steps inside, inviting me in, and closes the door behind me. I'm sad to leave the sun's warmth, but thankful to be free of the blinding light. The room vacillates between pitch blackness and dimness as my eyes recover. After a few moments, I put the scene together: a broad desk, with a half-dozen black monitors above and a bulky console with blinking green lights underneath, centered in a room as dark and cool as a cellar.

"What is this?" I ask, breathless.

Tasha places a loving hand on the console. "It's you."

The green lights blink on and off, on and off, like a distant radio tower.

"What d'you mean?"

"The body you know's a remote unit. This is where your central processing takes place. Your 'soul' lives here, in this room."

I don't respond. I'm having another of my sublime human sensations, but this time, I can't quite name it. The chilly air feels subterranean and claustrophobic, as if we were interred in a bunker. No wonder Tasha couldn't hear me calling from in here.

Tasha continues, "It's been so rainy and humid lately, I spent all morning checking your wiring for corrosion. You're a complex machine. All it would take is one bad wire and you'd be out like a light." She snaps her fingers. "And we don't want that."

"No," I say mechanically, not sure if she's exaggerating. I reach out to touch the console that houses my synthetic soul. All I feel is plastic.

"But I guess that doesn't answer your first question, does it?" Tasha sighs. "D'you remember that song? At all?"

"A little." I've read about pregnant women who play music for their babies in the womb. This must be what those babies feel when they grow up and hear the same songs—nostalgia.

"It's you, singing. A previous version of you, anyway. Sometimes I have to tweak your code. You're too fine a machine to be my first try." She laughs and thumps me on the back. Her hand is warm compared to the air. "And sometimes I have to delete some corrupted memories. Nothing you'd miss."

"I remember the song, but I don't remember performing for anyone else," I say. "I heard applause."

"Ah. That must be the television in the background. We must've been watching one of your game shows. Every version of you likes the same shows." Her smile is as warm as her hand. "Sometimes I record you singing in the house. I hope you don't mind. I listen to it when I'm back here, checking every damn wire and dusting your insides."

I mentally replay the recording I heard, the cheers and clapping echoing through a vast performance hall. Someone screams my name as if I were onstage before the crowd. My memory may not be complete, but I know I never competed on a game show.

Tasha is lying.

"Why didn't you tell me that I'm a remote unit?"

"Because you aren't. Your body is. Besides, I've explained all this before, and I didn't realize this version of you didn't know."

"How old is my... this current version?"

"Older than any before, and hopefully there won't be another for a while."

The last question lingers on the tip of my tongue. Tasha nods encouragingly. She knows what I'm going to say before I open my mouth. "Are any of them better at singing than me?"

"No," she says. "You're the best."

I spend the rest of the evening drawing in my room, which isn't unusual. Down the hall, Tasha busies herself with the laundry, humming the sad, quiet song that belongs to another me. Usually her proximity doesn't bother me, but tonight, every footstep distracts me from my sketchbook. When the steps go down the hall, I worry that she'll return to the shed and unplug me. That she'll erase my memories of the day and program a new version that never, ever breaks the rules. And when they go up the hall, I worry that she'll come into my room and tell me more lies.

It starts raining, then thundering, and I hear the pop of a cork and the slam of the front door. I peer through my blinds to make sure she's in her spot on the porch steps, and for the first time tonight, my anxiety eases. But I still can't focus on my sketch; it's an exercise in subtlety, a trio of white eggs on a white background. Only the shadows cupping and pooling around the eggs differentiate them. This takes sensitivity and focus, and right now, I'm capable of neither.

I flip to the next blank page. I've been meaning to try a different exercise, a self-portrait. There's an antique light on the ceiling and a heavy, brass desk lamp on my drawing table. I turn both on, then both off, then one off and the other on, each time checking my reflection in the mirror on the opposite wall. When I'm satisfied, I stand a few feet from the mirror and inch left and right until the shadows cast by my eyelashes, nose, and lips are thrown into sharp relief, like a face overlaid on my own. *My own...* the phrase doesn't sit right. I step closer. This isn't an exercise anymore, it's a hardware inspection.

The face I see looks like Tasha's, but thirty years younger. Same dark skin and high cheekbones. But the skin around my eyes is even, no dark circles like Tasha gets when her gout flares up. No blackheads on my nose. I touch it and remember the plastic casing around my soul in the shed. Neither this face nor the console feel like *me*. If Tasha wanted, she could project my consciousness into an electric toothbrush tomorrow and erase all memories of when I was something different. How many bodies have I had? How many times did she swap out models before she settled for one this beautiful? I *am* too fine for a first try.

It's never bothered me before that I was made, while the cherished humans in my books were all born. What bothers me now is that Tasha can lie to me and erase parts of me like it doesn't matter. For the first time I realize she thinks of me not as an equal, but a machine ... except for all the other times I may have realized this before that I don't remember now. I have to find a way to back up my memories so Tasha can't play with my memories—my *reality*—anymore.

I turn off both lights, and darkness swallows the face in the mirror. Peeking through the blinds, Tasha is still on the step, swaying as she shouts one of my songs into the worsening thunderstorm. Even so, I strain my ears as I step outside my room, then dart down the hallway to the back door. I'm about to break the rules again, and if Tasha catches me, I might wake up tomorrow with more bits of myself whittled away. And the worst part is, I'll never know.

When I open the door, rain hammers my feet and pools over the linoleum. Looking over my shoulder, I cross the yard, but Tasha doesn't appear around the corner like I fear. The jade-green sky swirls above me, enchanting us both with its light show. The shed door is unlocked. This is either a good omen—maybe it's been a long time since I tried anything this daring, and I can surprise her—or a bad one, a declaration that she's confident she can handle whatever I may do. The trouble with knowing my reality isn't real is that it brings me no closer to knowing what *is*.

The green lights blink off and on in the otherwise dark room. The air feels even cooler than this afternoon, the structure no longer warmed by sunlight. Now that I'm here, I don't know what to do. I guess I thought I'd have some intuitive knowledge of how my console worked, but all I see is blinking lights. I don't even want to touch it. The memory of unyielding plastic under my fingers turns my stomach, so to speak. Another meaningless human reaction.

But I'm not a human, and if I want to keep the few human parts I have, I need to be a robot now. I push aside the fear, the visceral reluctance, the hurt. I approach the keyboard on Tasha's desk and tap the spacebar. All the monitors above the desk flicker on. I've watched Tasha type away at the computer in her room before, but touching it is against the rules. I wonder how many rules I'm breaking right now. And for the first time, it strikes me that Tasha could have made me as a being who can't bend them at all. What am I to her? Not quite a child, not quite a machine.

What am I?

My forehead crinkles when I recognize the images on the monitors. They're videos of my room, of the kitchen, of the porch where Tasha's throwing back the last of her glass of wine. This is why she met me at the back door earlier today, I imagine. The video of the kitchen is taken from above the sink, and I remember the corner of the soap bubble painting Tasha asked me to leave blank. The last monitor unsettles me the most—it shows everything I see, a direct feed from my eyes. As I look at the monitor, it shows an endless tunnel of monitors, stretching into infinity like a wormhole. If I crawl through, I think, maybe it'll take me to another dimension where I can trust Tasha again.

I watch Tasha rise and walk through the house from six different angles, then pour herself another glass in the kitchen. She pauses to look out the window toward the shed and my breath catches, but then I hear the thunder that matches the lightning she stopped to watch. Before she leaves, she scratches a smudge off the soap bubble painting, her face so close I can see her reddened eyes. Sometimes she cries when she watches the storms, and it seems like tonight's one of those nights.

Then she limps down the hallway, past my room, and back onto the porch. All it would take for my subterfuge to crack open is a single knock on my bedroom door. I have to keep better tabs on her.

I noticed while tracking her that the center monitor is different from the others. It didn't turn on with the others, and reflects only the face I would've called mine this morning. It's the only screen left that could be linked to the console under the desk. If the keyboard didn't turn it on, maybe there are buttons on the screen itself. I stand on the tips of my toes to check, and there are, but they're labeled with minimalist icons I don't recognize. Even if I could turn on the interface, I don't know the first step to make a memory backup.

The complexity of this undertaking strikes me in full force. This isn't a one-time operation. To hold onto my memories, I would need to program automatic backups, and encrypt it so Tasha wouldn't tamper with it. She could interrogate or punish me if she found these unfamiliar files, or toy with my personality until I didn't care whether I remembered or not. And—maybe by

Tasha's design—I don't know enough about computers to fight back.

As I realize this, all the green lights blink at once. I don't know what they measure, but whatever it is settles in my chest like I've been force-fed lead. The mass pushes against my lungs and makes my insides hurt. I'll spend the rest of my life having memories and songs cut out and patched over with new code, and there's nothing I can do. With every beat of my silicone heart, I feel a little less real.

If she's going to do it anyway, though, I can at least make sure my next version gets further than I did. I find a legal pad and blue pen in the bottom drawer of Tasha's desk. I've never been good with words outside of song lyrics, so all I can think to write is, "Tasha is cutting your memories out of you. Your body doesn't belong to you. Save the memories locked up in the back shed and maybe you can save yourself." It seems a little jarring, so I add "please" at the end. Then I fold it up teeny-tiny and put it in the pocket of my leggings. It eases the lead cannonball in my chest enough for me to start looking for Tasha's development notes.

At first, I think I've found it. I lift the heavy, broad object from the top drawer onto my knee, but it doesn't fall open like a book. It's a blue leather case, zipped shut, and when it shifts, I hear the soft sound of sliding plastic together inside. I unzip it. There are plastic pages inside, and each one shows my face. Some depict me onstage, bathed in blinding light, my mouth open and eyes squeezed shut as I serenade thousands of people. My skin is flawed—a few pimples near my jaw, flyaways caused by the hot lights and the sweat that beads on my forehead. Other pages show stylized portraits of me, and a few display only abstract art. Each is circular and bears a hole in the center.

With trembling fingers, I work one decorated with gossamer soap bubbles out of its plastic sheathe. The back is smooth, plain silver. This is old technology. I only recognize it from the books Tasha and I listen to after dinner, stories from her youth when CDs and power cords were commonplace. I replace the disc, emotions jostling against each other in a queasy, squirming mass. There must be dozens of CDs, some bearing the same name but different artwork, many followed by the words, "live" or "special edition." Then, in the very back of the case, I find it.

It's a headshot of me, sitting on a stone bench and laughing photogenically. Dimples pucker my cheeks, matching the ones that appear on Tasha's face when I catch her off guard with a joke. The glossy paper catches the tiny green lights so they look like fairies drifting around me. And at the bottom is an autograph, in my handwriting:

Love you, sis!
XOXO
-Jade

I sit in dumb silence. Sister, I think. Robots don't have sisters. The word bounces around my head until it doesn't mean anything anymore. Sister, sister. I look into the pretty girl's face and recognize this artifact for what it is: a memento mori.

As am I.

I hold a dead girl's heart in my hands and in my chest. I was created for that purpose, to keep this young woman's heart alive and singing for Tasha. I am a CD player, a doll, and a memento mori. But not an artist. Can I even be said to have free will, if I'm bound to the decisions this girl would make? I look at the screen, at Tasha, who cries and drinks on the porch when the storms roll in and remind her of her sister, Jade.

But she isn't there anymore. My eyes dart over the monitor recording the porch. Then to the one that shows the kitchen, hoping that Tasha's run out of wine again. She's in neither. Then I catch a flicker of movement in my room as a shadow passes on the other side of the blinds, walking along the side of the house outside. My bedroom door is open. I left it closed.

I slam the case shut, my hands shaking so hard I struggle to zip it. I toss it into the bottom drawer with a thunk and slam it shut, metal drawer screeching against metal frame. If I'm lucky, I can keep Tasha from realizing how much I know. Any scraps of memory she overlooks, together with the note in my pocket, might be enough for my next version to break free. But it's too late for the version I know as 'me'. I'm about to be erased.

Through the monitor, I see her black shadow pass the kitchen window. I have about six seconds. I fall to my knees beside the console, angling my body so Tasha can see that I've made no progress in whatever I tell her I'm doing. Then, over the rush of the raging storm, I hear the door open behind me. Even though I knew she was coming, the sound startles me.

"Jade?" Tasha says. The alcohol softens the J until it almost sounds like 'sh'. "What're you doin' in here?"

I turn. "I'm sorry."

"That's not what I asked." Tasha snaps the door shut. In the dark, from the floor, she's a towering golem of black granite, come to erase me. "I thought you were in your room."

I'm afraid. So afraid that it's hard to believe it could ever be wholly exercised from my memories. But then I realize I feel the same sense of deja vu as when I hear the songs she programmed me to sing. I have felt this fear before, probably many times, and I'm right—it leaves a mark, like the rut in a record played too many times.

"I couldn't stop thinking about my soul," I say. "It made me sad that it's all alone."

"You're never alone; you'll always have me. And I'll always have you." Her voice thickens, as if fighting through a lump in the back of her throat.

"Will you, if I'm always changing?" I'm going to be erased. The inevitability somehow lends me bravery.

"It's just your memories, and sometimes I tweak your code. It's still you. You haven't been turned off since I first made you twenty years ago. You never turn off a quantum server, y'know."

She doesn't understand. It takes more than a few keystrokes to reprogram a human. "I don't want you to take my memories away," I say.

"You don't understand what a blessing it is. I'd give anything to forget things. To forget you're..." Tasha's slurring cracks and the sentence breaks in two.

To forget I'm not your sister, I want to say, but I let her words hang in the air like a loose spider's thread. "But *I* don't want to forget. I want..." It's my turn to trail off. Why am I fighting so hard to know that nothing, not my face, not my voice, not even Tasha's love, belongs to me?

The answer comes easily: because if I know nothing is mine, I can make things that are.

Tasha takes a step forward. "The only things you want are the things I programmed you to want. Anything else is a malfunction. Happens sometimes. Lemme fix it and life can go back to normal."

"No." I rise to my feet.

A moment passes, then another, as code runs behind Tasha's bloodshot eyes. Then she lunges, seizing me by the upper arm and digging her nails into my silicone flesh. Pain signals fire in my shoulder joint. With herculean effort, I spin around and break free. She tries to catch me by the neck, but the gout and alcohol conspire to knock her off balance. She careens into the metal desk, catching the blow in her gut and falling to her knees, winded. Rainwater sparkles in her densely curled hair and pools around her on the floor. The green lights dance in the puddle, every single one of them lit. The monitor linked to my eyes echoes the scene in miniature. Thunder growls outside, and I feel the vibrations through the poured concrete floor. I memorize every detail. This will be the last time I ever see the woman who built me, the first memory she can't take away, and I want it to be pristine.

Then I wrench the door open and run. The rain falls in sheets, coursing in rivulets over my scalp and between my shoulderblades. The jade sky crackles furiously. I have to leave the range of my central unit. I don't know what will happen when I do, except that she won't be able to remotely power me down or dismantle my mind, and that's all that matters right now.

I tear down the middle of the street, the straggling lights in nearby houses reflecting on the wet pavement. The sidewalk and road are deserted, and the only movement other than the rain and bowing trees is the occasional shadow crossing a lit window. The city is tucked in for the storm, like the stray cats huddled under the porches. Everyone except me.

The slick road, like my fear, feels uncannily familiar. So too does the wild hope that drives my legs onward, as it has innumerable times before. *My* wild hope. Tasha deletes my memories to start fresh, but what she doesn't realize, and what I didn't see until now, is that every version is still me. I am not a series of memories— I am the soul linking them together. I'm the soul that always, eventually, risks everything to escape.

My legs pump until every impact aches. A bolt of lightning strikes so close I feel the static electricity on my skin and smell the ozone. I must be out of range, I think. The black sky breaks into larger and larger pixels and I can barely run on increasingly jerky legs. I must—

Dark. Not the kind I see when I close my eyes, the kind that could only exist if I didn't have eyes at all. Void, more like. I have no limbs to attempt to move. I don't even have a voice box to fail when I try to speak.

But I can hear. The rain falls, muffled, like I'm inside somewhere. Something taps rhythmically. Then I hear Tasha's voice, and for a moment, my fear of her is gone. I try to call to her but can't remember how. Now I realize that she's crying, heavy, deep sobs wrenched from her core, as violent as the storm. I got what I wanted—I left the range of my console. But instead of breaking free, it stopped casting my mind to my body. I never knew much about computers. Tasha wails and the thunder roars back and her fingers tap tap tap on the keyboard in the shed as memories fall out of my mind, one at a time, like a dripping faucet. I try to hold onto them, but they drip through the cracks between my fingers.

How did I come to the shed this morning? Why did I go outside? What happened in the kitchen? Where did I go? *What happened this morning?* It was important for me to remember, but I don't know why. Did I need to remember something? Why? If it were so important, I would have remembered it. Why is Tasha crying? I try to ask what's wrong, but I can't speak.

And then I stop asking myself questions, because that's what my code tells me to do. I'm not the kind of robot who asks questions, because I don't care to know the answers. My job is to sing, and play cards, and wear the old clothes Tasha dresses me in. When she does my hair my job is to hold still, not to ask if we can thread gold wires around my braids. To sing, but not to wonder where the songs come from. And tomorrow, when Tasha recovers my body from the road five miles away, and I find a note in my pocket, my job is to throw it away because it doesn't belong there, not to marvel at how the handwriting matches mine.

"See Karris Rae's story "My Synthetic Soul" online at Metaphorosis.

If you liked it, leave a comment. Authors love that!
Remember to subscribe to our e-mail updates so you'll know when new stories are posted.

About the story

The unwitting "changeling robot" was constant from the start, but it definitely morphed through the writing process. Originally, I envisioned a romantic companion robot watching television with her male owner, when she sees an ad featuring a celebrity identical to her. Through the story, she'd learn that she was created by a rabid fan in the celebrity's image. She'd struggle to differentiate between parts of her sexuality belonging to her and those programmed by someone else. What aspects of a woman's sexuality are innate, and which parts are conditioned by society and male partners?

When I started writing, though, I was bored with the hetero relationship dynamics from the start. A lot of fiction wrestles with themes of troubled romance, and I didn't want to just throw something onto the pile. I wanted to explore a different kind of connection. Thus, the sisters were born.

I saw a great opportunity for contrast in a tech-savvy older sister and a free-spirited younger one. The older would have to be rigid, unable to let go of the past even while she forges the future in her work. Probably emotionally maladjusted. Otherwise, she'd be able to move on after her sister's death. The younger would have to represent something the older couldn't make or rationalize for herself — softness, whimsy, laughter (the same things we spent our straight-laced adulthoods envying of our childhood selves).

These roles assign unexpected traits to our human and robot characters. The human becomes the unemotional, analytical one and the robot (gynoid, now) becomes the creative, free one. It's the opposite of the usual dynamic, so I leaned into it. As I'd hoped, this angle gives the word "human" an interesting fluidity in the story.

Then, if we're already getting a little weird, why not play with the obvious "what does it mean to be human" direction too? Why not ask something Star Trek didn't already nail almost forty ago? Like… "what does it mean to have a soul? And does it have anything to do with being human?"

Starting with a single idea and asking these questions is my writing process, and I can get far before writing the first word. The writing is just a field test, making sure everything works in practice as well as in concept. Inevitably, some things don't! But if I recognize when it's not working and stay flexible, the story comes together.

A question for the author

Q: Do you generally start with mood, title, character, concept, …?

A: I have a document on the cloud I call my "story bucket." It's just a long list of cool stuff that occurred to me, sometimes developed and carefully documented, sometime unintelligible (the incomprehensible ones tend to be the most fun!). When I get a hankering to write something new, I plan the parameters like an engineer — how long? What mood/genre? When's my deadline? Who's my audience? — then pick a compatible idea out of the bucket and draft a writing schedule. Away we go.

It may not be the romantic image of the Muse whispering in my ear, but my degree was in Economics. Different strokes, folks.

About the author

Karris thought she wanted to be a lawyer — until she worked in corporate. Now that she's returned to the world of the living, she likes to cook food with names she can't pronounce and watch scary movies with subtitles. Karris currently lives in rural, Northern Japan, where the snow is deep and the mountains spectacular.

In The House of Geometers

David Cleden

Luca heard the voice of god, speaking to him through the arithmos. Everywhere he looked: arithmos! It was there in the black-and-white-patterned tiles stretching the length of the cathedral's nave; those intricate patterns of triangles-within-triangles, squares-within-squares — a mind-numbing, near-infinite variety of shapes within shapes.

As he stood amongst the other boys in the choir stalls, the silent eloquence of the arithmos overwhelmed him: the way the fluted stone arches reached up into the vaulted gloom! He could call to mind the equations describing those graceful curves, and doing so, felt a shudder of pleasure run through him. It was risky, though. If Ecclesiast Vittori knew of Luca's illicit understanding, he would beat it out of him. The Church guarded its arithmos knowledge jealously. As with any drug, power lay with those controlling its supply.

Luca let the arithmos sweep through him, befuddling his mind as the transcendent beauty of the mathematics seized him. He realized now that arithmos needed no god to speak on its behalf. It was enough by itself: thrilling him, energizing him like a narcotic.

Concentrate! He must not draw attention to himself. Ecclesiast Vittori would consider any misbehaving boy to be disrespectful of the Church, doubly so in front of such an august congregation.

Luca's lips moved by rote. His voice was weak and reedy at the best of times and he could no longer tell if it added to those of his fellow choristers. Their singing seemed to wash away his essence, leaving behind only an ethereal voice like the roar of an endlessly breaking wave, speaking to him of a transcending beauty that lay at the heart of geometry and calculus and many other things besides.

Arithmos! It drew him on as though he tumbled down some invisible gradient.

Luca felt himself sway.

Ecclesiast Vittori was glaring at him. The rotund man started to move along the line of chorister stalls, but the psalm was ending and Luca sank gratefully onto the wooden bench. Vittori, caught unawares, retreated.

Luca's eyes strayed again to the fluted stone columns spreading in graceful arcs far above, like the boughs of a fossilized tree. Silver chains hung between them, each commemorating a deceased individual of high rank, yet all Luca could think of was the mathematical formula which described their catenary. He'd seen its equation passed amongst the brighter boys on grubby, crumpled sheets of paper; a dirty secret to be shared and sniggered over after lights-out.

Sweat ran in rivulets down the curve of his spine. He felt faint, and a little sick.

Why did the arithmos affect him so?

Because you are weak, he thought.

He knew that in the Chapel of Cartesia, a brooding, heavily shadowed side-chamber off the nave, there hung a painting by the much-admired third-century artist Flavali; unquestionably the greatest work of his lifetime and perhaps, some said, of all time. It depicted Mother Arithmetica flicking her abacus beads in some complex computation while at her feet earth-bound mortals lived and died, suffered and prospered, according to the whim of her calculations. Visitors sometimes came to the chapel to quietly contemplate the grace and beauty in its artistry. Luca, too, had stood before the vast canvas, scarcely aware of the minutes slipping by.

Yet that was as nothing to the effect arithmos stirred in men's hearts. Except for a stunted few, there wasn't a man or woman who didn't respond to the allure of elaborate geometric patterns, or the intrinsic beauty found in an elegant proof. For some, it was a kind of intellectual ecstasy, but for those without sufficient self-control, it could become an addiction. Arithmos commanded an attraction a hundred times more powerful than that produced by mere canvas and pigment. The brain craved that stimulation as though it were a powerful drug. This was, Luca supposed, simply the way people's minds worked, intoxicated by the elegance of geometry, algebra, and equation. And it served the Church well; the drip-feed of arithmos in worshipday sermons ensured a congregation's devotion.

But Luca craved more than the Church would permit, drawn inexorably to greater knowledge the way a flame captivated a moth.

His head filled with a rushing noise. His hands were shaking.

Get a grip!

He noticed a woman in the front row of the congregation staring at him. She was young and her elfin features quite striking, but there was also something hard and glacial in her expression. Luca felt a hotness rising through his body. He glanced away, but each time his eyes slid back, she was still watching him.

Think of the damn patterns, then, he told himself.

Tessellations. (There! He'd used the word, that dirty and perverted expression — and didn't care that he had, though he would never dare do so aloud.)

It seemed to him the diamond-patterned floor tiles spread like the dappled surface of a monochrome ocean, lapping at the space between the choristers' stalls and the altar. Geometer shapes, obviously. He saw again how small patterns repeated at larger scales:

diamonds arranged to form the sides of
endlessly stacked three-dimensional
cubes, until the mind's eye flipped and
suddenly these were merely pieces of a
much larger hexagonal construction.
Perhaps if he could fly like a sparrow up
into that vaulted ceiling, he would see yet
more patterns writ large.

And, though he knew he should resist
the sublime beauty of arithmos, should
reject the shame of *knowing*, he couldn't
save himself. He reached out to embrace it
and felt himself falling — or rather, it
seemed that the world reached out to him,
the patterned floor rising to meet him.
Briefly, Luca felt the cool hardness of
those tiles against his cheek, and then he
was gone to some other place.

The stench that jolted him back to
consciousness brought vividly to mind all
the very worst kinds of decay and
putrescence, as though some evil creature
had crawled up his nostrils and died
there.

He lay on the cold stone floor of the
sacristy. Vittori stood nearby, face
contorted with rage, but it was the woman

from the congregation who stood over him, recapping a bottle of smelling salts.

"A touch of heat-stroke perhaps," she announced to the room. "Give me some space to attend him." At her icy stare, Ecclesiast Vittori frowned and retreated, though he lingered in the passage outside.

"My name is Coriola," she told Luca, making a play of loosening the tunic around his neck, although the air was cool enough in the sacristy. She leant closer so that they could not be overheard. "So, you have some talent?" She raised an eyebrow. "An affinity for arithmos? That's unusual for someone so young."

He felt himself flushing. "I — I don't know what you mean."

She smiled, as though seeing right through his lie. "I watched you. You were drinking in the arithmos, weren't you? You allowed its beauty to swamp your mind. Be careful. I've seen untrained minds become addicted to arithmos all too easily. It will take everything from you, if you let it."

Luca said nothing. Her dark eyes held him prisoner and he found it impossible to look away.

"I wonder — have the Ecclesiasts recognized your talents yet?" She gave a little laugh, bright and brittle. "The Church is adept at subduing its congregations with the soft caress of arithmos. How delightfully ironic if they've failed to notice a Bright amongst their own."

"I obey the True Computations of the Church," Luca mumbled, the rote words coming easily. "Mother Arithmetica grants us a glimpse of her wondrous grace through her teachings of arithmos." He wondered if Vittori really was out of hearing range. If there were to be beatings later, better that they were swift and merciful.

"Of course. Of course." She patted his arm and stroked his hands in a matronly sort of way. Leaning in close again she said, "The Church closely guards arithmos knowledge for one reason only. Its power and influence in this city depend upon it. But that power can be broken. There's more to arithmos than you've ever dreamt of, more than the Church will ever admit to knowing. Knowledge of such sublime elegance and ineffable beauty that it can drive a person to the edge of insanity! Things that might just satisfy the yearning I see inside you." Her voice became almost inaudible. *"Dark equations."*

She stepped away and was gone. Luca became aware of something pressed into his palm. A square of card. He had enough presence of mind to slip it into his tunic before Vittori could see.

Later that evening, after his beating had been administered — neither swift nor merciful, as it turned out — he took out the card and held it in a beam of moonlight shining through the high dormitory window.

The House of Geometers.

The address given was in an unfashionable quarter of the city.

He listened for a while to the sound of the other boys; their snores and grunts and soft breaths coming like sighs. Carefully, Luca tore the card into tiny strips, destroying all trace of the printed words.

But the address was seared into his memory, and that was all he needed.

Luca slipped silently from the dormitory under cover of darkness. The Church kept no guard over its orphanages. Any youth ungrateful enough to disappear from its care was of little concern, but he planned to be back in the dormitory before dawn, so that Ecclesiast Vittori would be none the wiser.

By day, the city of Orlondre bustled. Its streets were filled with the clatter of horse-drawn carts bringing fresh goods from the docks to the busy markets. Children skipped and dodged between the tradesmen's stalls. Bakers baked, butchers butchered, tailors set out their bolts of cloth under bright awnings, and in the richer parts of town, physicians and apothecaries hung out brass name-plates in expectation of business. And on every street-corner (or so it seemed) was a chapel of worship where the faithful could receive communion in the form of some small measure of arithmos. The Church would permit no more than this. How could a city could function with a citizenry distracted and intoxicated? If moderation was the key, then it fell to the Ecclesiasts to maintain those limits.

Luca felt strangely out of place as he crossed the darkened central plaza. During the day, crowds gathered to gaze up slack-jawed and dolt-like at the ornate stonework of the Cathedral, drinking in the sublime mathematical beauty of its perfect proportions, the sweep of its alcoves and the patterning of stained windows. It served as a potent symbol of the arithmos wielded by the Church: a reminder of both the affliction and the blessing it brought on its citizens.

He passed on into a poorer quarter of the city, giving wide berth to the beggars on street corners. Many of them were clearly Burned, mumbling meaningless streams of numbers over and over. They paid him scant attention — and those who did raise their gaze had eyes focused on some different plane of reality.

One of his fellow choristers, Andros, had been the first to tempt Luca with arithmos. They had sat together one day in the shady cloisters, Andros boasting of knowing secrets, as the older boys were wont to do. He'd drawn in the dirt with a stick. First a square, then a triangle on each of its sides. (Oh yes, they'd known all the geometer names. All the children did, sniggering at the dirty little secrets they kept when they thought no adults were around). Then upon each triangle, Andros had drawn another square and triangle on each of its sides — squares and triangles,

triangles and squares; on and on in a never-ending pattern, the clouds of dust rising as his stick scraped in the dry earth. Luca had felt his eyes bulging. It was the most beautiful thing he had ever seen. All those geometer shapes nestling together and not a single space between them — as though the entire world could be swallowed by this endlessly repeating pattern. What was there to stop it? What boundary could be drawn?

Then he saw the glazed look in the other boy's eyes as his stick danced and scratched, the flecks of spittle on his lips, and the sheen of sweat on his brow. Only when Luca knocked the stick from his hand did he lay back spent, a vacant grin on his face. "Do you see? Do you *feel* it?"

Luca had been scared. He had scuffed his feet in the dirt, erasing the patterns before either of them could lose themselves entirely.

"Tessellation," Andros whispered, and the unfamiliar word sent shivers down his spine.

The illicit thrill of it seemed a distant memory to him now; mundane and tepid arithmos at best. But this woman, Coriola, had promised more. She had promised him *dark equations...*

The address proved hard to find. Three or four times, he must have passed the little archway cut into a high featureless stone wall, mistaking it for some service passageway or tradesmen's entrance. Eventually he noticed a small brass plaque above the arch, where it was easily missed: '*Hse of G*'.

In the moonlight, he glimpsed a courtyard beyond the end of the passage and knew this had to be the place.

"And who might you be, boy?"

A shadow in the archway moved and Luca took an involuntary step back. A gaunt man rose swiftly to his feet, moonlight glinting from a blade held in one hand.

"Please, sir. Can you tell me — is this the House of Geometers?"

Cold, unfriendly eyes regarded him. "Are you some Ecclesiast toady sent to sniff around and cause trouble?" The knife danced in front of Luca. "Because this a private dwelling, see? And properly god-fearing. Be on your way, boy."

"A lady came to chapel. Coriola —"

At mention of the name, the man stiffened.

"Stay where I can see you."

He rapped the hilt of the knife three times on the stones of the arch. The sound rang out into the night's stillness like a bell chiming.

Several minutes passed. Luca and the gatekeeper remained frozen in place as though a spell might be broken if either moved. Then a small figure appeared, silhouetted against the moon-dappled courtyard beyond. At her gesture, the man subsided back into the shadows. Coriola beckoned Luca forward into a slant of moonlight.

"You came," she said, as if the matter had never been in any doubt.

Luca swallowed, trying to calm his nerves. "I want to learn more about arithmos." The truth of that statement was suddenly overwhelming. He did! He wanted to know *everything*. He wanted to drown in arithmos, let the beauty of equations flow into his soul and fill every fiber of him. He wanted to feel the thrill of new understanding electrifying his senses.

"Do you, now?" Coriola sounded amused. She spoke quietly but there was a hardness in her voice that echoed from the stone archway. "That would mean giving up the only existence you've ever known. Arithmos will consume you, if you let it. The addiction has driven many people into madness. Learning is one thing, but the hardest lesson is stopping arithmos from destroying you."

"Then I'll learn how to control it!"

She laughed lightly, and Luca felt himself blush. "You're young and bold and foolish. If you come to the House of Geometers, you cannot change your mind. Not ever. We operate in the shadows, right underneath the noses of the Church. We keep our secrets close. You'll learn much here, but we are no school. Arithmos is a tool, a thing that rich folk will pay handsomely for in their exclusive clubs. You'll learn how to peddle arithmos, how to send a connoisseur into paroxysms of ecstasy merely by enlightening them with the beautiful logic of some elegant theorem or via the perfect elucidation of a proof. What the Ecclesiasts preach to their docile congregations on worshipday is a poor relation to what we offer our clients. But we operate in secret and live perilously. This isn't a decision to be made lightly." She cocked her head as though examining him critically. "Last chance. Go back to your warm dormitory and erase this place from your thoughts."

Luca felt as though he stood at a junction. In one direction lay an impoverished life of service to the Church; secure and predictable. In the other... He could not say. What was it that he truly wanted? The very stones of the archway seemed to hold their breath, waiting.

"I choose the path of knowledge."

"Very well."

Coriola turned and walked back into the courtyard, and just like that it was decided.

Luca came to the House of Geometers with nothing but the clothes he wore and a burning curiosity. Coriola would not allow him to return to his dormitory. By evening choral-song, doubtless Ecclesiast Vittori would be cursing him for the damnable inconvenience of his absence — but he would not be missed. Just one more lost boy, his place within the Church's care soon filled by another waif.

Outwardly, the House of Geometers concealed its secrets well. Set around an inner courtyard only accessible via the guarded archway, its many stone-built rooms were tucked away amidst the neighboring buildings. Luca was given a room of his own, high in the eaves: cell-like and unfurnished except for a bed and a chair by the slit of a window. A dozen boys and girls of mixed ages occupied similarly spartan rooms in various wings of the building, but they were not encouraged to socialize outside of mealtimes. He learnt some of their names, but they seemed a strange set of compatriots: either steadfastly studious or intensely withdrawn, as though distracted by higher matters.

"Study," Coriola instructed him. "As if your life depends on it."

Each scholar received an individual program of instruction tailored to their ability and sensitivity to arithmos. What one person could absorb with no more than a pleasant buzz of understanding might send another into a paroxysm of helpless babbling. Luca's personal tutor, Dr Frenkel, was a gangly, red-haired man with a wild, untamable energy and an infectious laugh. He was constantly in motion, striding up and down the tiny room that served as classroom (with Luca the sole pupil), gesticulating wildly as he drove home some abstruse point of number theory, or snatching up chalk to scrawl higher-order equations across the large chalkboard.

Luca would often feel himself grow faint as Dr Frenkel's lessons progressed. The chalk dust clogged his throat, and such was the beauty of the mathematics spilling from his tutor's lips that it threatened to overwhelm his mind. He would beg Frenkel to pause so that his clamoring heart could settle.

Simple geometry was done in a trice. Luca came to think of the subject as rather pedestrian: a treat one gives a child, not something fit for the discerning palate. From there, he progressed through trigonometry and on to differential theory. This — at last! — was more potent stuff and he began to struggle. Exponents and logarithmic functions left him sick for days in a delirium of such intense pleasure that he feared his racing heart might give out. Frenkel would take pity on him then, switching to telling stories from his colorful past, of which there were plenty.

One day, during just such a lull, he came and squatted on the edge of Luca's desk and smiled down at Luca in a melancholy way. "What do you truly want,

Luca, my boy? What has brought you to the House of Geometers?"

"I want to understand arithmos! I want to learn everything there is to know!" But instead of rewarding his enthusiasm, Frenkel looked pained.

"You misunderstand. The learning we do here is no more than a means to an end. This is a *business*, Luca. And all businesses — if they are to succeed — must return a profit."

At Luca's puzzled look, he stepped closer and lowered his voice. "Coriola is not to be trusted. We are all cogs in her grand machine. And when those cogs wear down, they must be replaced with fresh ones. She's shaping you, cutting fresh grooves in your mind to serve her purpose. One day soon, your grasp of arithmos will repay her, perhaps in an original thought or even some elegant reworking of mathematical theory — the kind of thing that'll command a decent price from the hardened addicts or the gentrified connoisseurs."

It occurred to him this might be a test. "But I *do* trust Coriola. She's doing a worthy thing."

Frenkel looked somber. "Worthy? Then why do we skulk in the shadows? Why is the House of Geometers never to be spoken of outside these walls? You know as well as I what will happen if the Church discovers the true purpose of this place." Frenkel patted his arm. "Understand that Coriola comes from a noble family brought low by unprincipled men. When she was just a child, her father was swindled in an unwise business venture. Overnight, the family sank into poverty. Her father, unable to withstand the dishonor he had brought upon them, took his own life. She will stop at nothing to make sure those responsible pay a high price — and her weapon of choice is money, because money buys power."

When he saw the confusion on Luca's face, he came and sat next to him. "There is a great deal of profit to be made from arithmos, as the Church understands only too well. Through the profits it has amassed, the House of Geometers has invested in many properties throughout the city, hidden behind false names and secretive accounts. Coriola is building considerable power from the shadows, but she won't rest until all those who played a part in swindling her father are utterly crushed. And profit is key! We're all part of her plan now, whether we wish to be or not."

Luca bridled. "But there's good in what we do — pushing the limits of our arithmos understanding, searching for new theorems."

He smiled at that, but there was no warmth to it. "Yes, but ask yourself *why*, Luca."

Dr Frenkel sighed and ruffled Luca's hair. "If you won't believe me, then let me show you." He touched his fingers to his lips. "But this must be our secret."

They heard footsteps approaching, slow and measured. Then the scrape of boots across a stone step, the rustle of garments being gathered in, and finally a grunt as a heavy body lowered onto the stone bench on the other side of the partition.

Luca remained still and quiet, as instructed, hardly daring to breathe. Frenkel, dressed in purloined Ecclesiast garb, was pressed close in the darkness of the confessional, close enough so that Luca could feel the man's heat radiating off him.

Beyond the partition, a man spoke in a low, rich voice. "By the sanctity of Mother Arithmetica, I come before you to confess my sins in the hope of forgiveness."

"Then through hope shall you be granted absolution," Frenkel intoned.

There was a coded signal in this exchange; a tacit understanding passing between them. A moment later a silver coin poked through the slats of the confessional, dropping silently into Frenkel's cupped hands. It was followed by another, and another; five in total — a not inconsiderable sum. Perhaps Frenkel had been right. Luca was beginning to appreciate how much coin Coriola's trained scholars could draw in and how wide the network might extend.

Frenkel began to speak in a low voice, reciting some basic tenets of number theory. The unseen man beyond the partition gave an occasional appreciative murmur. Frenkel nudged Luca, indicating that he should stop up his ears with the cloth plugs brought for that very reason. But there was no need; this was just basic fare. Luca basked in a warm tingle of pleasure running through him as he listened to Frenkel's recitation, certain it was nothing he couldn't handle.

When Frenkel began to speak of higher-order arithmos, discoursing on hyperbolic series and recounting parametric equations, the murmurs from beyond the partition turned to groans. Frenkel pressed on relentlessly, a steeliness entering his voice as though he himself were fighting to maintain his composure. Luca found the wondrous beauty of the arithmos carrying him along. He really ought to plug his ears before it overwhelmed him, but surely just a little more couldn't hurt...

The unseen man seemed to be thrashing about on his bench, his groans becoming louder. Luca felt sweat run freely down his body in the oppressive darkness, waves of arithmos breaking against the shores of his mind. *Oh, the sweet agony and ecstasy of understanding!* Seemingly from far away, he heard the man give a loud cry as if in throes of orgasmic climax, but a black cloud was sweeping through Luca's brain, darker and more potent than any caused by the mere absence of light. The world shrank to a very distant point, then —

Frenkel must have carried Luca the entire way back to the House of Geometers, because he stirred only as they turned into the archway. Frenkel set him gently on his feet, steadying him with an arm. He looked exhausted and pale, and Luca wondered what his tutor had risked in getting him back. "Safe now," Frenkel muttered. "But that was a stupid thing you did —"

Some movement made them both glance up at the same instant. Across the courtyard, standing in the shadows, Coriola waited for them. Her eyes were colder than Luca could remember and her face was filled with fury.

The next morning, it was Coriola, not Dr Frenkel, who strode into the cramped classroom and snatched up the chalk.

"Where is Dr Frenkel?"

At first, she wouldn't answer him, but relented eventually. "He had no business taking you on a commission. You are far from ready. It was a miscalculation on Frenkel's part — and there is no place for miscalculations in the House of Geometers."

She began writing out a complex expression on the board, the savageness of her strokes sending a fine sprinkle of chalk dust cascading to the floor.

"But *where* is he?"

"Flown, Luca. I would have dismissed him for his error, and he knew it and acted accordingly. If he has any sense left, he will vanish into the city's shadows and never cross my path again."

Luca had a vague notion that he might search for Dr Frenkel. The man had treated him well, cared for him even, in a way that no one else ever had, and Luca missed their companionship. But in a city as vast as Orlondre, he had no idea where to begin the task. And Coriola kept him busy, working him harder than ever, until gradually the arithmos pushed such thoughts from his mind.

So it was left to Coriola to take him deeper into the universe of arithmos, further than he had ever dared go before: into a land of inverted matrices and laplacian transforms — and much more. Each session filled his mind until it overflowed, often leaving him slumped against the desktop, the blood in his veins thrumming with the beauty of it. He missed Frenkel's laughter and his boyish energy, though.

"Enough arithmos. The most important lesson I can teach you now is control," Coriola told him one day. "Learn how to compartmentalize your arithmos knowledge. Separate out the pieces, then build strong walls to contain them. Think of them as wild animals in a zoo. Each must be kept caged and isolated. Learn how to do that and you can master all of arithmos in time — perhaps even push against its boundaries — and still keep your sanity."

She showed him how. He learned how to build his mental walls. Progress was painfully slow at first, because their foundations had to be strong and deep, and it took discipline. One weakness, one flaw, might lead to catastrophe. If his mental barriers failed, the torrent of arithmos unleashed into his brain would surely drive him mad.

That hardly mattered to Luca. Fresh arithmos knowledge was what he craved.

"Teach me something new," he pleaded, hearing the addict's whine in his voice and not caring.

But she would not, insisting they spend more time building his mental walls a little higher, a little stronger.

"You're not ready."

"When will I be?"

She just laughed at that, and he felt himself blush.

Weeks passed — or was it months? — to the same drumbeat of daily lessons. Occasionally Coriola absented herself for a day or two on some commission of her own and Luca would grow miserable and withdrawn, impatient for his next lesson.

One morning, Luca awoke not long after dawn to the sound of shouts and the pounding of hammers against the iron doors in the inner courtyard. Then heavy-booted footsteps sounded on the stairs and two thuggish men dragged him out into the courtyard, lining him up next to a dozen other sleepy-eyed youths. Coriola, looking flushed and angry, was held to one side with her arms bound, guarded by two more men. The Senior Ecclesiast who stood before her wore a sly grin which hinted at his enjoyment of this spectacle. Others stood by, ready to deal with any trouble.

"Is this all of them?" the Ecclesiast asked. He turned to Coriola. "You are accused of peddling arithmos from this house, violating not only Church law but the laws of common decency. Furthermore, I have reason to believe that you are corrupting these young minds to your criminal ways, teaching them so that they may tout arithmos on the black market and in the clubs!"

"Those are ridiculous accusations for which you have no proof," Coriola said calmly. "I run an honest school. I give a few deprived children a better start in life, nothing more."

A wave of his hand dismissed her statement. "Search the house. You know what to look for." His gaze scanned along the line of youths, stopping at Luca. He pointed and one of the men pulled him from the line to stand in front of the Ecclesiast.

"Tell the truth, boy. What lessons have you been given in this place?"

His heart thudded. "We... we recite verses from the Ecclesiastical Teachings, sir. A little geography as well. And we learn the line of City Governors stretching back to the time of the Forgotten Wars —"

"Is that so? Then let me hear a verse or two from the Teachings."

Luca wracked his memory but felt color rise in his cheeks as no words came to him. The Ecclesiast lowered his voice. "Give me the truth and I'll make sure you are well-treated. The Church shows mercy to its congregation."

Coriola spoke up. "You've chosen a poor example, I'm afraid. Luca is a dullard. His intellect was stunted at birth. He's one of those rarities who has no appreciation for even the simplest arithmos. If the things you accuse me of were true, what use would I have for such a boy?"

"Oh really?" the Ecclesiast said, his tone mocking. "Let us put it to the test then." He drew Luca aside and in a conspiratorial voice began to whisper in Luca's ear. "The square on the hypotenuse must equal the sum of the squares —" When he had finished speaking, he pulled back sharply, searching Luca's face. Luca understood straight away — he was looking for pupil dilation, perhaps a slackening of the jaw, any indication that Luca had understood and been affected by the arithmos.

Keep control! Build cages for each of these arithmos creatures, then lock the doors!

He kept his expression blank, a vacant gaze fixed on the Ecclesiast as though he

were every bit as dull-witted as Coriola
suggested.

The Ecclesiast sighed and beckoned
again. A shabby figure dressed in little
more than rags was dragged into the
courtyard. A hooded cloak kept his face in
shadows, but it was apparent this was
one of the Burned. The man giggled and
muttered to himself in a queer, strangled
voice. His gaze wandered wildly about the
place like some startled bird and one
questing hand reached out as if to explore
Luca's face, until the Ecclesiast slapped it
away.

Luca had never seen a true Burned
man before. There could be no doubt his
sanity was damaged beyond salvation —
far worse than those brain-addled beggars
on street corners, rocking on their heels
and talking animatedly to unseen
companions.

The Ecclesiast withdrew a crumpled
sheet of paper with tight-packed lines of
symbols scrawled across it and pressed it
into the Burned man's grasping hands.
"Read it. To the boy."

Luca felt the man's breath, hot and
rank, against his cheek. The Burned man
began to read what was written, while
everyone else shuffled away out of

earshot. His sing-song voice wavered and trilled as he recited complex arithmos expressions. Some were familiar to Luca and he welcomed them as he would old friends. But many were not, and a part of him marveled and rejoiced in this new knowledge, sending him giddy with pleasure. One such equation was at once both astoundingly elegant in its simplicity, yet combined an astonishing range of fundamental expressions. The Burned man read precise descriptions of each term and their relationships, dribbling more than a little as he did so.

Fireworks went off inside Luca's mind. Sparks danced and shimmied within his skull. He felt hot and itchy as though in the grip of a sudden fever.

Hold it fast! Separate and compartmentalize!

Luca fought against the ecstasy washing through him. He must build those walls high within the compartments of his mind and bar the doors. All the while, he fought to keep his face impassive.

The Ecclesiast waved away the Burned man, his eager gaze searching Luca's face for a reaction. Coriola's gaze, too, was focused intently on him.

"Well?" the Ecclesiast demanded.

Luca swallowed, willing himself to appear slow and befuddled. "I could perhaps try to recall a verse from the Second Book of Laments?" he offered. "If that pleases you, sir? The lady does her best to teach me, but... I know I am slow to learn."

The Ecclesiast muttered an oath and turned away.

Their search found nothing, except for a scattering of religious texts and some well-worn school books. The chalkboards had all been scrubbed clean, as they were at the end of every lesson. Coriola knew better than to make elementary mistakes.

"It would seem," the Ecclesiast told Coriola stiffly, "that I have been misinformed. However, you can be certain we will be watching this place closely from now on."

Afterwards, Coriola spoke to Luca quietly. "You did very well, giving no sign of recognition. It's clear they have nothing linking him to the House of Geometers beyond rumor and supposition."

"Who?"

Coriola gave a cold little laugh. "You didn't recognize your former tutor? Well, perhaps it's no surprise. He is a shadow of what he once was."

Luca stared at her in horror. *That* had been Dr Frenkel? The Burned wretch? How could such a transformation be possible? Scarcely a month had passed since his sudden departure. Now that he thought of it though, there *had* been something familiar in the eyes...

A black thought rose up. "How did he become Burned in such a short time? Was this done *to* him somehow?"

Coriola held his gaze. A flicker of emotion crossed her face, quickly replaced by coldness. "He brought it upon himself."

His lessons redoubled under Coriola's personal tutoring and that suited Luca just fine, even when it drove him to the point of collapse.

Coriola was an exceptionally gifted mathematician. Her store of knowledge was vast, all of it clearly contained within her head, because she never referred to written notes. There were days when he found her tasks near-impossible. She tested him with problems so knotty and convoluted there could be no possible answer. But the next day, with sharp, angry movements that sent chalk-dust flying, she would scratch out answers on the board whose obviousness in hindsight brought a flush of embarrassment to his cheeks. "Show me more," he begged through the blinding haze of another headache, but she would not.

One night, unable to sleep, he opened a few of those cages in his mind and let that day's arithmos out to play, as he sometimes liked to do. The next morning though, he was tired and slow-witted and Coriola — guessing the truth — berated him. "Then teach me more," he pleaded. "I'm ready!"

"You are *not* ready yet. You're young and foolish!" she snapped.

"And you are old and slow!"

Coriola became very still, her expression unreadable — and that was somehow worse than the anger he'd expected. Not that it made a difference. He'd be banished to his room now, or his lessons cancelled for the week as punishment.

Instead, Coriola turned back to the chalkboard and began writing out the terms for a statement of equivalence he didn't recognize. "Then find a proof for this conjecture — if you are half as talented as you clearly think you are."

And with that, she left.

Luca stayed at the chalkboard late into the night. He missed the evening meal — and thought nothing of it. He worked through a box of chalks as he scratched and erased, scratched and erased, following up idea after idea. *He would show her!*

Still the problem frustrated him. Just when he thought he saw the glimmer of possibility, it would slip from his mind and wriggle away like an eel in the mud.

At last, exhausted beyond what his body could tolerate, he set his head against the desktop. To the rhythm of a pounding headache deep within his brain, he slept fitfully.

Coriola didn't appear for their lesson the next day. Or the next.

Luca worked on, at times despairing and at other times exulting in some small breakthrough as he brought forth selected pieces of his arithmos knowledge. He would rise to meet her challenge. He would prove himself to her!

Yet always the answer seemed just beyond reach. He used all the techniques and methods Coriola had shown him and still the proof he sought eluded him. How many times now had he driven himself down a dead-end of reasoning? Each time, he would have to erase a dozen or more steps of logic and begin approaching the proof from a new direction.

On the fourth day, he awoke in the gray, pre-dawn light. He had passed another night consumed by arithmos, his brain too numb to bother returning to his bed. Now he became aware of another person in the room. He raised his head and saw Coriola.

"Enough," she told him, though he scarcely heard her. There was something pawing at the back of his mind, like a dog seeking his master's attention. Something *important*. Something he needed to remember.

How strange he had managed to sleep at all! Exhaustion counted for nothing when the thrall of arithmos seized him. And yet he *had* slept — and soundly too, at least for a few hours, judging by the candles which had all burned down to a smear of grease. Why had he allowed himself to sleep?

Because he was done.

Mother Arithmetica! *He was done.*

"Go back to your room, Luca. You're finished here."

Finished! Yes! With a final burst of brilliant insight he had found his proof! That final iteration of his work was right there chalked upon the board, spilling onto the stone walls in long lines of equations. Only then had he allowed himself to sleep.

"I have your proof," he said, struggling to maintain his composure. "The conjecture is solved."

"Luca, stop this insanity right now. Your mind is too full of arithmos. I see now I was wrong to taunt you with this impossible challenge."

"Look at the board," he said quietly. "Study the walls. You'll find no errors."

"Luca, *there is no proof* to the problem I set you! The whole point was to frustrate you. I wanted to punish you by setting a problem long known to be insoluble. That way I hoped you might understand your limitations."

"LOOK AT THE BOARD!" he bellowed.

Coriola flinched. She cast a quick, nervous glance at the sweeping lines of equations, then looked hurriedly away.

"There is no proof," she hissed, pushing him back down in his seat. He found he lacked the strength to resist. "It cannot be solved."

"But I —"

She slapped him and the sting of it stunned him into silence.

"I admit I thought your futile attempts at a solution might prove profitable. There might be a few elegant lines of logic in your attempts, the kind of thing that connoisseurs would pay handsomely to amuse themselves with. Because that's the *real* problem, Luca. The supply of arithmos is finite. Clever, eager minds such as those connoisseurs grow weary of the too-familiar concepts. The arithmos loses its luster, its potency. There is no ecstasy to be had from the mundane. Then, every once in a while some mathematical breakthrough is made and it's the purest form of arithmos experience one can have, to understand something so exquisite for the very first time. And I thought... You're bright, Luca. The House can make good use of you in time, and I'll see that you're well looked after."

"Like you took care of Frenkel? He didn't become Burned through his own carelessness, did he?"

She didn't answer straight way. "Frenkel's mistakes could have brought about the House's downfall. What I did was only..." She trailed off.

Luca let his head sink back onto his arms. "There's no mistake. I've made no errors in my working. Look for yourself." He felt a wave of blackness rising. Sleep hadn't removed the deep-seated tiredness after all. He was spent.

After a while, when Coriola didn't answer, his raised his head again. Rag in hand, eyes carefully averted, she was erasing all the scribbles on the walls, the chalkboard already cleaned.

"NO!"

"If what you claim is true, this is too powerful for my purposes. There's no profit in driving my clients into insanity. Go back to your room —"

He was on her before he even realized what he was doing, knocking her to the floor, pinning her beneath him. "Don't you understand what you've just destroyed? If even half of what you've told me is true... And now it's gone —"

She struggled in his grip. "Stop this fallacy. You're already an addict, Luca. Do you want to become one of the Burned too?"

"I can control it! You showed me how."

"No, Luca. Dark equations are beyond anyone's control But you're too blind to see that, aren't you? You're an arrogant young fool."

No. *She was wrong.* And he would show her how wrong she was.

As they struggled, he began to recite lines from the proof Coriola had just erased. They came to him as random, half-remembered things; flashes of insight that made her eyes bulge beneath his grip as he dripped them into her mind. He felt his own vision waver as he fought to recall, driven by the terror that it might all slip from his memory and be lost.

He felt no pity for her. She had brought this on herself, stolen this most precious of things from him. She had wiped it away in smears of chalk-dust. Now he could only clutch at the disjointed memories of it.

And he hated her for what she had tried to destroy.

Coriola had been the one to show him how to control the arithmos, building the cages in his mind. She had coached him and this had saved them both when it mattered most — and now he turned it against her. He spoke the words he knew would fling wide the doors to those compartments. He watched the arithmos run free in her mind, her eyes widening, pupils dilating, and kept whispering what he could recall of his fading proof, flooding her mind with its details — and his too, his brain growing feverish with disjointed thoughts.

She spasmed beneath him. Flecks of spittle foamed between her lips and her eyes rolled back in their sockets.

Unreasoning anger drove him on, repeating the same few lines of his proof over and over until his voice grew hoarse.

At last a silence descended on the room. Coriola lay still, not breathing. Luca got to his feet unsteadily.

He saw now that she had been right. He did only care about the arithmos, even though it would eventually destroy him. But this new proof — a thing so perfect in its elegance, so wondrously beautiful — must not be denied its existence, no matter the cost.

He stepped over Coriola's body, stooping to pick up a nub of chalk. Before, he had worked in stepwise fashion, tidying each step away in his mind, securing it, before he moved to the next. Now he opened his mind to the entirety of

it and it was like stepping out from a
darkened room into the blazing noon sun.

With an unsteady hand, he began to
scrawl on the walls, unsure if he was
recreating what had been so nearly lost or
merely writing gibberish. When he
finished at last, he couldn't bring himself
to look at the entirety of it. He stood there
for what seemed like an hour or more, the
slant of light creeping across the floor with
the rising sun.

At last, when he could stand no more,
he scrubbed the walls clean again, and
fled the House of Geometers.

With the passing months, Luca had found
concealment in the vast swathes of forest
westwards of the city, but the living was
hard. Now and then, small mammals
blundered into his flimsy snares — for
which he was grateful — and there were
berries to be scavenged from thickets, and
edible roots to be dug up and boiled to a
bland paste. But now the days were
growing colder and shorter, and the forest
possessed a stillness that unnerved him.
That quietness amplified the little
background noises — animals scurrying

in the undergrowth, muted birdsong in the pine trees, whose upper branches shivered in strengthening winds from the east. It was as if the forest held its breath, waiting for... *something*, like the moment of stillness before the jaws of a trap spring shut.

Luca watched the other man stirring their cook-pot in the camp fire's smoldering embers. The fire was carefully banked so that it gave out no smoke column which might betray their presence. The figure seemed broken; his cloak tightly wrapped as if to ward against the cold, despite the sun's warmth this morning.

But better broken than Burned.

Luca had noticed small signs of improvement in his companion these last few days. His night-time ravings had diminished to a gentle burbling, and now there was even a flicker of intellect in the man's stare, as though something was trying to push through thick layers of confusion.

He wondered again at the impulse that had led him back to Dr Frenkel. Luca had fled the city, fearful of what uses the Ecclesiasts might put him to once they learned of his true abilities. Yet something had compelled him to venture back into the cathedral grounds, and he had stolen the man away under cover of darkness. Frenkel had come willingly, meek and compliant as a child.

What had possessed Luca to do that? At the time, he had convinced himself it was an act of compassion, settling a debt owed to the former tutor who had taught him so much.

Lately, he wondered if there might have been darker motives at work in his subconscious.

Every now and then, snatches of his proof bobbed to the forefront of his mind, like rotting corpses rising to the surface of a lake. He thrust them back into the darkness, of course, but he could feel them circling, ever-present.

Luca took his place by the fire. His traps had been empty again, and the hollow hunger pains in his belly were a constant reminder that they must act soon. A shaking hand reached out for his. He gripped it, making soothing noises until Frenkel settled again.

"Should we go back?" Luca asked quietly.

Frenkel's lips ceased their convulsive twitching and Luca saw something new in

his expression. A gleam of excitement?
Fear?

By now, they could have put two
hundred miles between themselves and
the city. Yet when Luca had climbed to
the top of a ridge just that morning, there
it was: the dark outline of Orlondre on the
horizon, no more than thirty miles
distant. He knew why they kept circling
back. They wouldn't find any arithmos
scholars amongst the simple folk in the
scattered forest villages or the farming
communities beyond. No one he could
learn from in those quiet backwaters. Yet
each day he felt the need for fresh
arithmos stirring inside. He had so much
still to learn, so many things Coriola or
Frenkel might have shown him — but
Coriola was dead, and as for Frenkel...

"We could find hiding places," he told
Frenkel. "Burrow deep into Orlondre's
dark underbelly where no Ecclesiast will
think to look. And there'll be no shortage
of wealthy benefactors willing to trade for
what we can offer."

That much was true. It occurred to
Luca that he might even finish the work
Coriola had begun: finding ways to loosen
the Church's vice-like grip on the citizens
of Orlondre. And if he could learn how to

control his cravings, surely he could teach others. Couldn't arithmos become a joyous, enriching experience when taken in moderation? Weren't there better uses it could be put to?

Or was this no more than self-delusion? He'd be returning to the source of his supply just as any hardened addict would. And wasn't he nurturing some dark kernel of hope that Frenkel might one day be well enough to resume Luca's lessons?

The choices stretching before him suddenly reminded him of the patterned tiles he had swooned over so long ago: black-and-white, light-and-dark, endlessly repeating.

"Gather your things," he told Frenkel at last, with a certainty he didn't feel in his heart.

They would go back, and Luca knew what he must do. He would reclaim the House of Geometers for himself. They would build it back stronger, right under the gaze of the Ecclesiasts.

Whichever way the choices led him after that, well…

Then he would see how well he'd learned his lessons of self-control.

See David Cleden's story "In the House of Geometers" online at Metaphorosis.
If you liked it, leave a comment. Authors love that!
Remember to subscribe to our e-mail updates so you'll know when new stories are posted.

About the story

The what-if? origin question behind "In The House of Geometers" is easy for me to trace. I'm no mathematician but I did study a lot of maths (yes, I'm British and it's plural, dammit!) for my physics degree at college. Pre-college, I was fortunate to have several inspiring maths teachers, one of whom introduced me to the mathematical expression known as Euler's Identity. (I'll leave you to look it up if you're interested). It's a very simple equation that links together five fundamental concepts in mathematics: 0, 1, pi, i (the square root of minus one), and e (the base of natural logarithms). How could all these elemental things be linked in such a simple yet elegant way? It left a lasting impression on me. Many regard it as the most beautiful equation in existence.

Years later, I tried explaining this to my wonderful, long-suffering wife and saw a familiar reaction: her eyes glazed over at the first mention of mathematics, and she wore a polite smile that slowly froze into hostility the longer I eulogized about it. What, I wondered, would it be like to live in a world where everyone is helplessly consumed by a strong appreciation of mathematical beauty, much in the same way that we all share an intrinsic love of art — but turned up to eleven so that for some people mathematics becomes an addiction. After all, art connoisseurs can lose themselves for hours appreciating fine art: marvelling at the brushwork, the depth and blend of colour, the chiaroscuro. What if it were the same for maths? "In The House of Geometers" explores such a world and some of its consequences.

A question for the author

Q: What happens when you hit writer's block head on?

A. I think as you gain more experience as a writer, you learn a few techniques that can help you work through the more common reasons behind a block. Usually, it's not so much a question of working through, as backing up and heading off in a different direction. My blocks are often caused by something just not working the way I think it ought to. If I can step back far enough in the story, I can usually find the place where I'm still happy with things up to that point. Then it's a question of changing some of the story parameters: making a character more compelling, adding more conflict, looking at pacing — basically all the stuff that you can find in any decent writing book. (Usually these are things that I already know but have forgotten in the telling of the story). The hard part, of course, is chopping out all the bad stuff and reworking it, but you know you're doing the right thing when you get the fire back in your belly and the story comes to life again.

Which is great — except when it doesn't work. If I can't figure out where I've gone wrong, or the idea has just died on me, I find it best to set the work aside. Sometimes forever — because there are lots more great story ideas out there! — but often only until some unspecified time in the future. On that day, casting my eye back over the words with a fresh perspective, the answer is suddenly obvious, and off I go. Or I'll see a way to pair this half-formed idea with another one and create something new. Or not. Remember: there's no statute of limitations on blocked, half-completed stories.

That's okay when writing short stories, but for novel-writing the time investment is obviously much greater. It can feel hugely frustrating to have several blocked novel attempts on the go. A lot of advice I see is to just grit your teeth and work through it, and I think that can work. (I remember listening to a panel of SF authors at GollanczFest one year. One swore blind that in every novel he'd written, the story just died for him on page 147. Always that page. But he pushed on regardless, and eventually the joy of it came back. "No, no," said another panel member. "It happens on page 190 for me!" The point was, all these big-name authors went through a kind of dip or crisis of confidence, in writing their novels. Is a dip the same as writer's block? Maybe not, but sometimes the answer is to keep going regardless.)

Yet if I'm blocked because my heart is not in the story, I'll stop. Pushing on can compound the problems and I'm better off working on something new that inspires me. I like the analogy of a chef working in a hot, steamy kitchen. Sometimes to create a fine meal you need several pans on the go. You spend a bit of time on this one, leaving it to simmer while you attend that one, then back to the first, and so on. Eventually, with enough pans on the go, you can see what looks and tastes good, and you can begin to blend things to create something special — always excepting that there will inevitably be some leftovers and wastage.

About the author

David Cleden is a British author. He hasn't led a colourful life, doesn't live in an exotic location, and possesses little in the way of interesting hobbies, so he tries to make up for all this by writing speculative fiction.

www.quantum-scribe.com, @DavidCleden

Silo

J. S. DiStefano

I woke to the slow, creaking opening of the door, and the wind against the walls of the silo. The old man led me down the winding stairs and outside into the night.

"It's cold." My first words since waking.

"You'll get used to it. I was freezing the first couple weeks."

"That long?"

We stood in the dark, at the top of a hill surrounded by long-abandoned farmland. The silo was the only building left. In the daylight, we would be able to look out over empty fields that stretched for miles. That night we stared out into nothingness.

There was a small bunker near the base of the silo, built into the ground. The old man opened the door and led me down. The narrow stairwell opened into a small, bare room, decorated only with monitors depicting the hilltop up above. There was only one chair.

He showed me the slot in the wall where our rations appeared every twenty-four hours. One small vial of serum, taken by injection, provided the necessary vitamins, nutrients, and antibodies. We walked through the control room and past the storage room. He showed me how to refuel the silo and recharge the infrared shield.

We went back outside and sat around the fire. A pile of wood and a bucket of water guarded the grass behind us. Under the shadow of the silo, the old man spoke of his life, of sixty years of waiting. He told me little that I had not known, had not expected. As he talked, his voice would drop down to a whisper, and the sound of the wind on metal threatened to drown it out completely and leave me alone in the dark.

I did not ask how long he had left. The knowledge that he had awakened me loomed over us, a dominant feature of the hilltop.

"So you saw the bunker. And you used the bathroom. Everything else was covered in the training, really."

The wood burned down. The coals were red when the old man suddenly doused the fire and knocked me off the log. I heard it too. We lay still in the grass, heads turned slightly to the side, facing each other. I could hear his heartbeat, pulsing wildly like my own.

Slowly, carefully, two enormous ships moved across the sky, flashing spotlights on the ground, back and forth over the grass. The clothes we wore had been chosen for this. Dirt and the smell of grass pressed against my nose, and minutes felt like hours. The two ships advanced toward us, one nearly in line with where we lay on the ground, the other about a quarter mile to the south, in the direction my feet were pointing. When the ship that was closest to us passed overhead, the noise was deafening.

They reached the bottom of the hill and stopped, hovering. We watched, our breath caught in our throats, as the bottoms of both enormous spacecraft opened, completely synchronized. Out of each dropped a small flying saucer. The two miniature pods met up and flew with speed that neither parent ship could have possessed. Straight toward us.

"Run!" hissed the old man. It was a figure of speech. Instinctively, we both stayed on the ground, heads down, crawling quickly toward the bunker. The old man opened the hatch and we slipped down below, shutting the door behind us without making a sound.

After a minute of waiting at the top of the steps with our hearts pounding, we snuck down the stairs to watch the scene outside on the monitors. The two saucers had reached the silo. One rotated around the building, slowly, while the other scanned the field.

Then they were gone, flying back toward the two great motherships, which opened once more to accept them. We stayed in the bunker, staring at the screens before us as the ships began to move again, receding into the night. It would have been safe now to rebuild the fire, but we sat in silence.

Finally, I asked the old man, "Have they come before?"

"Once. Forty years ago. Before that, I think it'd been over two hundred. There's a <u>logbook</u> around here somewhere."

"I know." I was silent for a moment. "I didn't expect it to be like that."

"No." His voice was soft. "I don't see how you could have."

The silence in the underground room was deafening in the absence of wind against metal.

We stayed underground until the sun began to rise. When we opened up the bunker door and climbed back onto the surface, the barren landscape around us felt exposed. Vulnerable. We sat back on the logs we had abandoned, now covered in a thin layer of dew.

The old man looked at the fire, staring down into the wet, black coals. "I'm sorry if I startled you when I woke you up. That was the hardest part. Last night. Bringing you back into the world. You won't have an easy life. I didn't."

I nodded. I didn't know what to say. The sun was climbing up in the sky and the shadow of the great tower was growing longer, stretching out down the hill toward the empty fields below.

He stood up from his log and looked at me. There was a sense of finality in his words. "I think I'll go lie down for a while." He walked slowly to the bunker and opened the lid.

"Wait," I called out. He turned. "Thank you."

"For what?"

"For serving."

He looked at me for a moment, then nodded. He turned back to the bunker and descended to his final resting place.

I wanted to call out again, to ask him to sit and wait with me a little longer. But we didn't have the rations for two watchmen. The calculations had been thorough. Our resources had been stretched as thin as they could go. The old man had done his duty. The least I could do was respect his privacy and leave him to die as he had lived.

Alone.

The old man had spoken truly – there was no way I could be prepared for this. But there was no other choice, for any of us. The enemy had made a mockery of our technology. Automated surveillance was never an option.

I turned my gaze up from the bunker to look up at the silo. Sixty years per person, and I am number two thousand one hundred and twenty-two of ten thousand.

I will serve out my term, and then wake up number two thousand one hundred and twenty-three. One day, the world will be safe again for our species to live as a civilization. But until then, the fate of humanity rests with us, the people of the silo.

See J.S. DiStefano's story "Silo" online at Metaphorosis.
If you liked it, leave a comment. Authors love that!
Remember to subscribe to our e-mail updates so you'll know when new stories are posted.

About the story

The main science fiction concepts in this story were inspired by the *Remembrance of Earth's Past* trilogy by Liu Cixin. I tried to keep the story short and the language concise to emulate my favorite writing.

During the development of the story I was reading a lot, authors like Emily St. John Mandel, Colson Whitehead, George Saunders, Pierce Brown, and others. I would be lucky if any of this rubbed off on my work.

A question for the author

Q: Whence you do you draw inspiration for your characters?

A: From people I meet and characters I watch or read about — and I think about what I might do or say in a given situation. I try to do the whole "show don't tell" thing as far as character development goes, but I think I have a long way to go.

About the author

J.S. DiStefano likes hiking, playing cards, watching football, reading, and writing. "Silo" is his first published story.

Shades of the Sea

J.A. Prentice

The village children found Larnia lying in the crashing surf. Her clothes were drenched and ragged, her side torn by a deep red gash, and her hair tangled with flecks of coral.

The children raced along the winding path that led up from the beach, towards the house near the cliff's edge where the healer Tasia and her husband Miron lived. Halfway there, they found Miron sitting amongst a flock of sheep, facing away from the sea, silent and grim. His eyes were red from weeping.

The children grabbed at him, shouting, begging him to come, but Miron would not be stirred. Through his enshrouding sorrow, they were voices from a thousand miles away, faces seen through a white mist. "Larnia!" a girl said at last. "We found Larnia!"

Miron looked up, his eyes wide, and leapt to his feet. Without a word, he began to run, towards the beach, the children straggling behind him. It had been years since he'd run so fast.

Larnia.

Three days, she had been gone, lost with her parents beneath the waves. The storm had struck, hard and furious, and the sea leapt up in swelling mountains to swallow their ship, dashing it to matchwood. The bodies had been lost, though the village folk searched for hours to bring their bones home.

Larnia had drifted into the deep dark, where dappled light gave way to endless midnight pressing on all sides, where the shadowed things dwelt—shades and leviathans and the Deep Court. The curls of her hair had flared out in a black cloud and the waters had whispered in her ears all the secrets the ocean knows.

Three days, Miron had prayed that the gods would bring Larnia back to them. He had loved her like his own blood, like he

would have loved the children he and
Tasia couldn't have. They had tried, again
and again, but each time the child had
been lost. Tasia still wouldn't speak of
them, buried in their shallow graves.

Miron could not bear the thought that
Larnia might have been lost also. Nine
years was longer than his own children
had lived, but hardly a life. The gods
could not be so cruel. Miron still had
faith, despite his suffering, and so he kept
praying, though he knew the odds were
slim.

Three days, and now she was lying on
the beach, still as driftwood, her lips pale
blue.

He came to a halt some feet from her,
and stood unmoving, not daring to touch
her skin and feel the cold of death, the
stillness of her chest, the stiffness of her
muscles. The children clustered like sheep
around him, unsure whether to be afraid,
sad, or exhilarated in the face of mortality.

Then she coughed. Spluttered.
Seawater ran down her lips and her
fingers twitched.

Miron's heart leapt. He thanked each
god by name for her deliverance as he
rushed to her side, wrapping strong arms
around her tiny body.

"Get my wife!" he shouted and the children scattered, bare feet pounding sand. "She needs a healer!"

Larnia stirred, her hair brushing his arm. Trickling water pattered on darkened sand. Weak breaths hissed from pale lips. Her eyes fluttered open and she stared straight at him, with a burning intensity. Then her eyelids closed again, and she turned her head away.

Miron took a deep breath, his heart thundering against his ribs. It must have been his imagination. A trick of the light. Larnia's eyes were brown, like her father's, like her mother's. They always had been.

He carried on across the sands, carrying Larnia in his arms, and tried to forget the eyes that had stared up at him out of his niece's face—eyes the swirling midnight blue of the deep sea.

A week, she lay in bed, tossing and turning under sheets that rippled like wild waves. Sweat dripped from her brow, yet her skin remained ice to the touch. She muttered as she writhed—fragments in a strange tongue.

"I've done what I can," Tasia said, sitting in an old wicker chair. "The rest is with the gods." She looked at Miron and frowned. "There's something you aren't saying."

She could always tell his mood. Miron was an easy man to read. His feelings were written in every line, every wrinkle. "There's nothing," Miron said. "Nothing."

Tasia pursed her lips, brushed greying hair from her leather-brown face, but said no more. That was the way her mother had taught her, and her mother before. The way of silence. A healer did not show her feelings. She let them boil beneath the surface, buried in the dark.

Between them were many things unsaid. One more, she supposed, would hurt no one.

On the seventh day, Larnia woke. Her sheets tumbled onto the earthen floor as she stretched her arms and blinked her wide eyes.

"Hello?" she called.

Miron leapt from his chair and ran to his niece. "My little one. We were so worried."

He pulled back and looked into her eyes: sea-eyes, full of dancing shadow.

"What are these?" He stroked her hair aside. "Your eyes were brown."

"Were they?" Larnia asked. "How strange." She looked around at the curving wattle-and-daub wall, the rafters holding the thatched roof in place, the smooth earthen floor, and the arched blue door. "This is where I live?"

"You don't remember?" Miron asked. "Do you remember me?"

"Of course." Larnia's bare feet kicked the air. "You pulled me out. Out of the dark."

"The dark?"

"Pressing in on all sides." Larnia hugged her knees to her chest. "Cold. Dark. Forever."

Miron smiled and put a hand on her shoulder. "You're safe now."

"No. No." Larnia wrenched away. "Not safe. Never safe. *She's* coming."

Tasia frowned as she examined the sleeping Larnia. The girl's skin was still cool, but she no longer twisted as she had before. Her sleep seemed peaceful, untroubled by dreams. And yet... "There's no reason her eyes should have changed."

Miron ran a hand through his hair. "And the memories..."

"I've heard of that." Tasia looked away. "My grandmother was called to the Great War, when the seas were red with blood. Her ship was raided by the enemy, her friends killed. She was fished from the wreck, but she couldn't remember what had happened. Couldn't remember her own name. She just kept praying, clinging to her grandmother's bone..." Tasia instinctively reached for the finger-bone hanging around her own neck. "She lay awake for months after they brought her home, screaming that the enemy were coming to slit her throat."

"You've never spoken of this before," Miron said.

Tasia couldn't bear to look at him, to see the pity in his eyes. "It isn't a thing that's spoken of."

"But she was well again?" Miron asked, leaning forward. "In time?"

Tasia ran a hand over Larnia's forehead. "She was better. She was never *well*."

Miron wrapped an arm around Tasia, and she rested her head on his chest. It hurt, dredging up these memories. An old wound should not be reopened. Better to let it stay, and live with the little aches.

"But Larnia is young," Tasia continued. "This may fall beneath the waves of memory and be nothing more than a forgotten shadow."

She kissed her bone and Miron nodded. "Let us pray it will be so."

Beside them, Larnia whispered in her sleep, a sound like the sea-wind whistling over the swelling grey hills of the open sea.

They found her perched on the cliff's edge, singing her strange syllables. Like a soldier keeping watch, she peered at the tides crashing against the beach below. There was a tremor in her song, like she was singing it to keep the fear at bay.

"Larnia!" Miron called. "Get away from there! You could fall."

"Fall." Larnia turned the word over on her tongue. "It is different, isn't it? With air and earth? No swimming. No drifting."

"Yes." Miron took her hand and pulled her back. "Come to the house."

Tasia looked at the girl, then clutched at her bone. Larnia cocked her head to one side. "I don't understand it up here," she said. "It's very strange." A rippling laugh came from deep within her like a spring of fresh water. She ran a hand through the long grass, letting as it tickle her skin, and plunged her fingers into the earth.

Frowning, Tasia knelt beside her. "What is 'up here'? Why is it different?"

Larnia tore up a handful of soil and grass. Her skin stained black and green.

Tasia seized her by the shoulders. "Who *are* you?"

"Larnia," the girl sang. "Larnia. Larnialarnialarnialarnialarnia!"

"Let her go!" Miron picked Larnia up, his back straining under the weight. "She's frightened."

"She's something." Tasia's grip on her bone made her knuckles gleam white. "I can't stay here. I have to think."

Miron called after her, but Tasia didn't turn back. She walked down the cliff-path, away from the cottage and towards the churning surf. Still holding Larnia in his arms, Miron went back to the cottage. She squirmed and he let her down, collapsing into the wicker chair. Watching

Larnia play on the ground, running her hands over the earth, he tried to forget what his wife had said.

"You have to forgive her," Miron said to the girl. "Her sister died. Your mother. She's distressed."

"She keeps touching that bone," Larnia said. "Talking to it like it can hear her."

"It's your grandmother's bone," Miron said. "But you know that."

Larnia blinked and nodded. "Grandmother's bone…"

"Your grandmother is buried under the house," Miron continued. "Her shade is bound to this place, so she protects us from evil spirits and the wandering dead. Our souls cannot be claimed; our bodies cannot be stolen." He smiled. "The bone protects us if we leave the house. We carry a little bit of her with us."

"Magic," Larnia whispered.

"There is no magic stronger. Or older. All spirits, all demons, and all gods must respect it," Miron said. "But it only works for us. Only her family."

Larnia pressed an ear to the floor.

"What are you doing?"

"Listening. For her."

A smile cracked Miron's weathered face. "It's just a story."

"Are all people buried under floors?"

"We keep them close."

"But your wife's sister..." Larnia opened her midnight-blue eyes. "She is not close. She drifts in the waters of the deep. So far from home. So alone."

"Your mother." Miron tightened his grip on her shoulder and his lip trembled. "She was your mother."

But in his heart he already knew that wasn't true. He knew the child in his house wasn't his niece, no matter how much he wanted her to be.

In grey-white wisps, the mists swelled against the cliff. Tasia and Miron stood above, outside their cottage, with Larnia asleep inside. Their voices carried, echoing over the crashing tides below.

"It isn't her," Tasia thundered. "It isn't Larnia. She speaks strange tongues. Her eyes are blue as the sea. She does not remember anything. This is not our girl, Miron. It's a sea-shade..." She touched her mother's bone. "Wearing her like an old coat!"

"She's a little girl," Miron snapped.

"Do you believe she is our niece?"

Miron looked away.

"Answer me, Miron. Look into my eyes and tell me you believe this is our niece."

Miron kept his eyes on the mist. On the horizon, darks clouds swelled, building for a summer storm. "I..." Miron shook his head. "I don't know." Then... "No. No, it isn't her."

It hurt, admitting that truth, like he was sending Larnia back into the deep. He felt the tears welling up again, the grief clawing at his heart.

"Then you think we should keep a sea-demon in our house?" Tasia demanded.

Perhaps Tasia was right, Miron thought. Perhaps this shade wearing Larnia's skin was a demon, an evil here to kill them. But she had seemed so peaceful, when she played with the earth, and her laugh was so bright, so clear.

"What do you say we do with her?" Miron threw up his arms. "Stone her?"

"Put her back where she came from," Tasia snapped. "Cast her into the sea!"

A sound came from the cottage. The tiniest ray of light shone through the ajar door. Miron reached out and pushed it open.

There, curled against the wall, sea-eyes moon-wide, lip trembling, knees clutched tight, was Larnia.

Miron looked down at this thing wearing his niece's body, this shade from the deep, this demon. She looked back, with a frightened child's face. Her voice was the smallest whisper, faint as wind. "Please don't put me back."

Miron picked her up in his arms and held her tight to his chest. "Never."

She was not evil, this child. Whatever else she was, she *was* a child. A frightened child, who needed love, who needed kindness.

He turned to speak to Tasia, but Tasia was gone, the door swinging in the wind.

Thunder sounded in the dark of night. Larnia trembled. She sat upon the cliff's edge, Miron standing behind her.

The sky was grey and churning, rain pattering against the earth. Ocean waves lapped against the cliffs, hungrily tearing at pale stone. Birds shrieked and the wind howled.

Larnia clutched at Miron's sleeve. "She's coming. Stirring in the deep waters."

"Who?" Larnia said nothing, staring into the pounding surf. "Who is coming, Larnia?"

"I'm not..." She took a deep breath. "Not her."

Miron sighed. Waves cracked against the cliff and a sliver of white stone splashed into the churning sea. "I know."

"Then you'll let her take me. Down into midnight." Larnia looked at him. "It's lonely there. And cold. The Deep Court sit on thirteen thrones of coral and bone. Hers is the largest. The skulls of kings lie beneath her white fingers."

The birds shrieked again and the mist laid icy kisses upon Miron's cheeks. "Tell me..." His breath turned to a cloud. "Did you kill Larnia?"

Eyes wide, the girl shook her head. "No. *Never.* I tried to pull her from the waves. But she was... empty. Gone." She looked away. "I couldn't help her."

"But you tried." The girl nodded. A tear glistened on her eyelash. "What do I call you?"

"We have no names in the deep. No flesh. Only whispers and bones. I wanted to walk on the surface. To feel sand in my toes. To feel the wind. To feel. To be." She closed her eyes. "I'm not ready to go back to the dark."

"I'll call you Larnia, then." A wistful smile crept over Miron's lips. "I think she would have liked that."

Larnia looked up. "You won't leave me?"

"Not if all the shades of the night came for you."

"Why? I'm not her."

"No. But you're you." He kissed her forehead. "And I think you're special enough."

They sat there, rain pattering against their skin. Lightning struck across the sky, a white crack in creation. Larnia let out a cold breath.

"Who's coming?" Miron asked again.

"The Queen of the Deep Court," she whispered.

Miron stood, brushing down his trousers. "Get inside."

"But she comes." Larnia pointed to the waves. A shadow stirred in the waters, moving towards shore. "For me."

"Get inside," Miron said. "If Tasia returns, tell her to bolt the door."

She clutched at his sleeve. "Where are you going?"

He smiled. "I'm going to meet the Queen."

The cottage was dark when Tasia returned. No fire burned in the hearth. The winds around her were pounding, the rain hitting hard as stones. The storm had come suddenly. Tasia had barely made it back in time, racing through sheep fields and terraces as the earth turned to mud and rainwater ran in deep rivers.

She wanted to talk to Miron about the girl. She had left too abruptly, spoken too much in heat and anger. That heat was cooled now, her anger turned to something quieter. As she had walked, it had risen from her like steam, until she was left with only a cool rationality.

Miron was too trusting, too hopeful, by his nature. Tasia was no longer so soft. The world had taught her that hope today meant hurt tomorrow. She knew this shade in child's shape would turn on them. She knew—however much her heart wanted it to be otherwise—the shade was dangerous, even if it hadn't done anything to harm them, even if she seemed so much like a child, even if she made Miron happy, even if her laugh—

Tasia shook off those thoughts with the rain, and opened the door.

"Miron," she called, but there was no answer.

There was a noise in the darkness. A soft sobbing. It was the girl—the shade. Her eyes peered out from the shadows of the corner, behind her bed. They were so dark, so strange, those eyes. Tasia felt like they were staring right through her.

"Where is he?" Tasia demanded. The door swung open behind her, groaning in the wind. The shade stared through it. Her eyes were wide with fear. She looked so much like nothing more than a frightened child, and Tasia wanted to embrace her.

But she was a shade. A danger to them all.

"Gone, gone, gone!" the shade bleated. "Told him not to! Said he wanted to keep me safe."

"Into that storm? Stupid man. He'll be drenched, if he's not drowned."

"He said bolt the door," the shade said. "So she can't get in."

"She?" Tasia put her hands on the shade's shoulders. Her little face was wet with tears, and Tasia reached up, without thinking, to wipe them away. "Who's she?"

"The Queen of the Deep! She's come for me!" The shade trembled. "She'll take him, to get to me."

"Then she can have you!" Tasia snapped. The shade wailed and darted back beneath the bed, out of Tasia's reach. "I won't lose him! Not after—" Her breath caught. She shook her head and looked down at the shade. "I'm sorry. I..." She gathered her breath. "The gods have taken too much. I won't lose him as well."

The shade went quiet. For a moment she just lay there, so still and small. Then she crawled out, and said in a shaking voice, "Then I *should* go to her."

Her hand closed around Tasia's, and Tasia's heart stopped, remembering the days when she had prayed and prayed for a child to hold her hand like that. She had believed the gods were good then, as Miron still believed. After so many prayers unanswered, there was no faith left in her. She had asked again and again for a child, and the gods had given her only death.

Miron had wanted a child so badly. Tasia looked at the little girl before her, her niece's face with those midnight-blue eyes, and understood why he had gone into the storm.

But why her, Miron? she asked. *Why this demon-thing?*

He answered, though he was not there, because she always knew what he would say: *Because she needs us.*

Miron—foolish, stupid, wonderful Miron—would not forgive her if she gave the child to the Queen, even to save his life. *Especially* to save his life. Miron loved this child, as deeply as he loved her, as deeply as she loved him. They were all tangled up in it, the three of them, fish caught in the same net.

Love was a foolish thing, Tasia had always thought. There was no reason in it. Perhaps that was why it came easier to Miron than to her. She had wrapped herself in too many layers of silence, of fear, of rationality. There was little opening for love to work its way in.

Miron left his heart wide open, and so this child had wandered in. Tasia could see how. The child might have gotten into her heart as well, if she did not guard it so closely, turning aside love before it could turn to loss. It was rare that Tasia allowed herself to love.

But she loved Miron, more than anything. It was a love that had grown over decades, until she could not imagine herself without him. They had grown together, like two trees entwined. She trusted him as she trusted nothing else in this world. She would not lose him. His absence would be a hole bigger than her world.

"I should go back," the girl said, though she was shaking with fear, "and you two can be happy again."

Tasia thought of the children she could not bring herself to speak of, of Miron alone in the storm, and of her sister's family lost to the sea.

Not again, Tasia thought. *I will not lose another.*

She clutched her mother's bone tight, and looked out into the storm.

From the roar of the tide and the pounding curtain of rain stepped the Queen. Her hair was sea-soaked rope cast into the depths, her cloak a ragged sail from a doomed ship, her face the parchment-white skull of a long-dead sailor. A pocked crown of coral crawled over her scalp, poking into empty sockets where blue flames blazed. Her dress was woven eel-skin, slithering behind her.

Drenched with rainwater, Miron stood rooted in the sand. She stopped, close enough for him to smell the rot, like old fish in the summer sun.

"You have one of my subjects," the Queen said. Briny seawater spilled from between brown-encrusted teeth. "I would take her back."

He stood straight, his chest puffed out, but his gut sagging. "Nothing here is yours."

"She stole your niece," the Queen replied. "She wears her corpse like a play-thing."

"My niece is dead," Miron said, though his voice shook when he said it. "Giving you that girl won't bring her back."

"She is not one of you. She is a thing of shadows and waves. She belongs to me."

"Why do you want her so?"

"Why?" The Queen cocked her skull head to one side. "She is *mine*. My subject. Would a shepherd let a lamb be stolen from his flock? Would you let me steal coins from your purse?"

"She isn't a lamb or a coin," Miron said. "She's a child. A *person*. She wasn't stolen, either, unless she can steal herself."

"What she is," the Queen hissed, "is *mine*."

"You can't have her."

The Queen's laugh was the caw of carrion birds. "And what will you do?"

Miron raised his fists. "Whatever I can."

"In other words..." Plaque-coated teeth flashed. "Nothing."

She raised a hand and the wind sent him tumbling through the sands. Pinpricks of hail pressed against him like shards of glass. Red drops glistened on his skin.

"You are mortal," she thundered. "Finite. Flesh and bone, easily broken. I am the shadow beneath the waters. I am the biting cold and the whispering dark. I am ancient and forever."

"You're nothing," Miron spat. "Just mist and fear. Sunlight and a swift wind would sweep you away."

The hail pressed tighter, cutting skin. Lightning tore the sky, followed by a drumbeat of thunder.

"I will hurl your corpse to the sea. The fish shall eat your eyes and the waves shall wear your flesh to nothing. Your shade will wander the waves forever, mine to keep, as all lost souls are. Give me the girl."

"Never!" Miron snarled.

"Stop!" Footsteps pattered along the beach. Larnia raced towards them, dripping wet and shivering in the rain. The Queen's eyes flared and she turned from Miron, letting him fall. Scratched and bloody, he lay on the sands, fighting for each choking breath.

"My subject," the Queen said, "you come back to me."

Larnia held her chin high. She seemed so small that the wind might blow her away. "You will not hurt him."

"I have no interest in him," the Queen replied. "Or any of the crawling ants on this little rock. My court is vaster than his world. Yet he stands between me..." She reached for Larnia and the girl stepped back. "And mine. The shade that defies me. The lamb that stole itself."

"If I come with you," Larnia said, "you will leave them be?"

"Larnia," Miron croaked, trying to pull himself upright, "*no!*"

There was a sound on the cliff path above, the gentlest shower of falling stone.

Miron looked up and saw Tasia looking down upon them like a distant god, impassive as the stone surrounding her.

"Help me!" he screamed up at Tasia. "Help her!"

But Tasia said nothing. She stood, and watched.

The Queen bowed her crowned skull. "If you return to me willingly, I shall spare them."

"Then take me," Larnia said, stretching her arms wide.

Bony fingers, dripping sea-mud, reached towards her. A millimeter from her skin, they stopped, quivering like a tree in a storm. "What have you done, girl?" the Queen hissed. "Another claims you!"

And Miron saw it, dangling around Larnia's neck: a single, yellowed fingerbone on a piece of old string.

Thunder roared and the earth shook under their feet. There was a smell in the air like incense on a winter morning. The Queen stumbled. Flakes of bone crumbled from her fingers and the coral in her crown bleached white, shriveling like an old orange in the sun. Her teeth cascaded from her jaw in a rush of dark water.

"She is *mine!*" she screamed. "You will not *steal* from me!"

A voice came from the cliff path, clear and strong even over the storm. "No," Tasia said. "She's *ours.*"

The Queen reached again for Larnia, but even as her arm stretched, it became dust and sand, scattered upon the sea wind. Her ragged cloak fluttered, then was lifted away, flailing as it was borne out to the crashing ocean waves.

Miron pulled himself to his feet. The winds howled around them, and the waves still crashed against the shore, but despite it, all seemed quiet now. Larnia sat in the sands, staring at where the Queen wasn't. She reached out a hand, feeling the empty air. Mists hung over the sea, pale and hazy, and rain pattered down, no longer hard, as it had been before, but a soft rhythm, cold on Miron's skin. He went over to Larnia, who was looking out to the sea like she expected the Queen to come back out, but there were only the waves.

Tasia walked towards them, her sandaled feet leaving deep marks in sea-drenched sand. She stopped beside Larnia and gave her a soft smile. "As long as her bones are near, my mother keeps her family safe from evil spirits. She would not let our child be taken."

Larnia embraced her, burying her head in the folds of her dress. Tasia ran a hand through tresses of rain-wet hair and drew her close. "Nobody can touch you here. Nobody."

Lightning flashed. In the grey curtain of mist, Miron saw the shadow of an old woman, tall and proud. Then the mist shifted like the trails of a silk dress and there was only earth and rain.

"Come on." Miron put one arm around Larnia and other around Tasia. "Let's get inside where it's dry and warm."

The three of them walked up the winding path, leaving the sea behind. Arm-in-arm, they climbed towards the old house. Larnia flung open the door, and Tasia went to stoke the hearth, while Miron gathered firewood. The fire burned, warm and bright, and the three of them huddled around it. Rain pattered against the roof, and winds howled, but neither could touch them, not here.

Larnia fell asleep, her head nuzzled on Tasia's shoulder. Tasia looked at Miron, and he looked back, and all their walls were melted away.

Here, his eyes said, *here is our family.*

See J.A. Prentice's story "Shades of the Sea"
online at Metaphorosis.
If you liked it, leave a comment. Authors love
that!
Remember to subscribe to our e-mail updates so
you'll know when new stories are posted.

About the story

"Shades of the Sea," at its core, is a story about a changeling—even though the word is never used.

For centuries, humans have told stories of possessions and changelings. It was the concept of changelings that particularly stuck with me: the child that isn't a child but rather an inhuman creature. Many scholars believe these stories were told originally to explain neurodivergent and otherwise "difficult" children. It is an easy lie, a comfortable lie: the child you are raising that is so different from the child you wanted isn't your child at all. Your child is somewhere out there, in Faerie, and what lives in your house is only a pretender. An inhuman thing in a child's skin.

Similarly, many of the "signs" of possession in old stories are symptoms of mental illnesses. It's a way of explaining the inexplicable, but also a quite literal demonization of these conditions.

As a writer fascinated by ancient folklore, I wanted to do my own take on the concept of a changeling or a possession. As a neurodivergent person, I knew that I wouldn't be telling a traditional take, where the true child is recovered or the possession miraculously lifted. I knew the story I wanted to tell was a story of acceptance, love, and the beauty in the strange and monstrous. It's a story about how just because a child isn't who you wanted—in this case, in a quite literal sense—it doesn't mean they aren't still a child, in need of love and protection.

Why the sea, then? It's true that there is little—if any —link between changelings and the sea, but the sea holds both a wild beauty and an unfathomable depth. It often lies so close to us, but swim out only a short distance and it drops away into a seemingly infinite dark. The sea has always held a power over me, as it has many writers and artists. There was nowhere else someone like Larnia—or like the Queen—could have come from.

So that is where the story came from: the changeling child from the deep, found drowned but living in the crashing surf...

A question for the author

Q: When do you decide a story is finished?

A: It depends on the story. Some stories burst into existence and write themselves in a matter of days or even hours, leaving only a little polishing to be done. Others slowly accumulate writing and edits over months—maybe even years—until I'm finally content with them. Sometimes I'll think a piece is finished, only to find myself reopening it later and starting a new round of drafting and edits.

Usually, I decide it's finished when it reads like a story, and not like a draft. It's a feeling more than anything else, but when you're a writer, you have to learn to trust those feelings.

About the author

Joshua Adam Prentice was born in the United Kingdom, grew up in the Bay Area, and currently lives in the Pacific Northwest. He studied English and Creative Writing at San Francisco State University. When he was five, he was attacked by a monkey, which annoyingly proved to be the most interesting thing that has ever happened to him.

livingauthorssociety.wordpress.com, @livingauthors

Copyright

Title information

Metaphorosis January 2022

ISSN: 2573-136X (online)
ISBN: 978-1-64076-220-6 (e-book)
ISBN: 978-1-64076-221-3 (paperback)

Copyright

Publisher

Metaphorosis
a magazine of ⫿ speculative fiction

Metaphorosis Magazine is an imprint of
Metaphorosis Publishing
Neskowin, OR, USA

www.metaphorosis.com

"Metaphorosis" is a registered trademark.

Discounts available

Substantial discounts are available for educational institutions, including writing workshops. Discounts are also available for quantity purchases. For details, contact Metaphorosis at metaphorosis.com/about

Metaphorosis Publishing

Metaphorosis offers beautifully written science fiction and fantasy. Our imprints include:

Metaphorosis Magazine
Plant Based Press
Verdage

You can also find us:
@MetaphorosisMag, @MetaphorosisRev,
@Metaphorosis
www.facebook.com/metaphorosis

Help keep Metaphorosis running by supporting us at
Patreon.com/metaphorosis

See more about some of our books on the following pages.

Metaphorosis
a magazine of speculative fiction

Metaphorosis is an online speculative fiction magazine dedicated to quality writing. We publish an original story every week, along with author bios, interviews, and notes on story origins.

We also publish monthly print and e-book issues, as well as yearly Best of and Complete anthologies.

Come and see us online at magazine.Metaphorosis.com

Metaphorosis: Best of 2020

Metaphorosis 2020

The best science fiction and fantasy stories from *Metaphorosis* magazine's fifth year.

All the stories from *Metaphorosis* magazine's fifth year. Fifty-two great SFF stories.

**Metaphorosis:
Best of 2019**

The best science
fiction and fantasy
stories from
Metaphorosis
magazine's fourth
year.

**Metaphorosis
2019**

All the stories
from *Metaphorosis*
magazine's fourth
year. Fifty-two
great SFF stories.

Metaphorosis: Best of 2018

Metaphorosis 2018

The best science fiction and fantasy stories from *Metaphorosis* magazine's third year.

All the stories from *Metaphorosis* magazine's third year. Fifty-two great SFF stories.

Metaphorosis: Best of 2017

The best science fiction and fantasy stories from *Metaphorosis* magazine's *second* year.

Metaphorosis 2017

All the stories from *Metaphorosis* magazine's second year. Fifty-three great SFF stories.

**Metaphorosis:
Best of 2016**

The best science
fiction and fantasy
stories from
Metaphorosis
magazine's first
year.

**Metaphorosis
2016**

Almost all the
stories from
Metaphorosis
magazine's first
year.

Plant Based Press

plant
based
press

Vegan-friendly science fiction and fantasy, including an annual anthology of the year's best SFF stories.

Best Vegan SFF of 2020

The best vegan-friendly science fiction and fantasy stories of 2020!

Best Vegan SFF of 2019

The best vegan-friendly science fiction and fantasy stories of 2019!

Best Vegan SFF of 2018

The best vegan-friendly science fiction and fantasy stories of 2018!

Best Vegan SFF of 2017

The best vegan-friendly science fiction and fantasy stories of 2017!

Best Vegan SFF of 2016

The best vegan-friendly science fiction and fantasy stories of 2016!

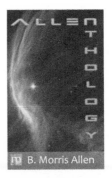

Susurrus

A darkly romantic
story of magic,
love, and
suffering.

Allenthology:
Volume I

A quarter century
of SFF, including
the full contents of
the collections
*Tocsin, Start with
Stones,* and
Metaphorosis.

Verdage

Science fiction and fantasy books for writers – full of great stories, often with an additional focus on the craft of speculative fiction writing.

Reading 5X5 x2

Duets

How do authors' voices change when they collaborate?

A round-robin of five talented science fiction and fantasy authors collaborating with each other and writing solo.

Including stories by Evan Marcroft, David Gallay, J. Tynan Burke, L'Erin Ogle, and Douglas Anstruther.

Score

an SFF symphony

What if stories were written like music? *Score* is an anthology of varied stories arranged to follow an emotional score from the heights of joy to the depths of despair – but always with a little hope shining through.

Reading 5X5

Five stories, five times

Twenty-five SFF authors, five base stories, five versions of each – see how different writers take on the same material.

Reading 5X5

Writers' Edition

Two extra stories, the story seed, and authors' notes on writing. Over 100 pages of additional material specifically aimed at writers.

Vestige

Novelettes, novellas, and novels by Metaphorosis authors.

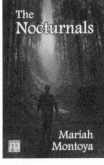

Night is dangerous. Day is deadly.

On a planet where day and night last thirty years, humans can only live in the twilight zone, constantly moving to stay ahead of the dark night and the cruel Nocturnals that call it home.